THE DEVIL'S HOLIDAY

Robert O. Harder

AmErica House
Baltimore

Copyright © 2000 by Robert O. Harder

All rights reserved. No part of this book may be reproduced in any form without written permission from the publishers, except by a reviewer who may quote brief passages in a review to be printed in a newspaper or magazine.

First printing

ISBN: 1-58851-353-X
PUBLISHED BY AMERICA HOUSE BOOK PUBLISHERS
www.publishamerica.com
Baltimore

Printed in the United States of America

DEDICATION

To my late mother, Myrtle Nelson Harder, who lived through the Columbus Day holocaust and encouraged the telling of this story.

Noon, Thursday, October 10th, 1918
The Northern Pacific Railway Depot
At Brainerd, Minnesota

KRIEG DABEK
Wanted For
UNSPEAKABLE ATROCITIES!
MURDER! JAILBREAK!

    Joe LaBounty held the hastily printed poster at arm's length, as if to distance himself from Dabek's snarling image. The photograph was of good quality but it did not come close to depicting the man; there wasn't a camera made that could capture the essence of Krieg Dabek. A body had to stand next to him, mark the way he moved, size up his incredible physique, smell his peculiar scent, peer into those opaque eyes, to have any notion not what Dabek was--not even Joe fancied he knew that--but *what you were up against*.
    LaBounty had picked up the flyer when he got off the train to buy a bag of peanuts. Dabek's bustout at Aitkin was big news; the waiting room passengers could not get enough of it. Nothing like a sensation, Joe thought, to set folks' blood to running, especially if it meant collecting on the pleasure so many get from someone else's troubles.
    LaBounty stepped up to his car still reading, having got down to the small print on the bottom. Aitkin County Sheriff Ike Boekenoogen was calling for temporary deputies to join in the manhunt. Which accounted for the unruly gang of young men that got on the train during the peanut stop.
    "We'll bring 'em in!" one suddenly said in a nervously loud

voice. The others slapped the fellow on the back in agreement, laughing and boasting as only the genuinely innocent could. Joe sadly shook his head.

The locomotive steam whistle shrieked twice and the train jolted forward. LaBounty settled in his seat and stuffed a handful of unshelled peanuts in his mouth. He kind of liked the taste of the shells and the way they crunched between his teeth. Besides, he was too hungry to bother husking the fruit from them. Joe made a ball of the poster and pitched it aside. Dabek wasn't his problem and he was powerful glad of it.

His hunger temporarily sated, he pulled a letter from out of his coat pocket. The paper was dog-eared and badly wrinkled from all the many times he had folded and unfolded it. He opened it slowly, using extra care on account of it was getting ready to tear apart along the crease lines. Slowly he reread the last words his mother ever wrote him.

She had been feeling poorly. Not in so many words, not in simple written sentences, did he know this. Mary LaBounty had never been one to suffer publicly what ailed her. She was of the type that bore pain stoically, almost proudly. Joe knew his mother was not well from the *way* she wrote. More slant in her letters, a certain wavering here and there, a failure to punctuate. He had known this the first time he read the letter. When she was still alive. When he might have gone on home and done something about it.

Aching bodies and tough conditions were nothing new for the LaBounty family. All the many years they had followed old Tom around from one lawing job to the next, the always pitiful pay that generally left them with one foot in the county poorhouse, the lack of any particular place where the LaBountys could call home, had left their mark. Even worse for Mary, after the boys had gone off on their own and Tom had passed, folks' true colors showed. She could not get fit work or find a decent place to live. Her health worsened. After a few years of lonely struggle, she gave up on the white world and returned to the Sandy Lake Ojibway. To where Tom and Mary had first met, back in the early frontier days, when a white man in the northern Minnesota woods was still a curiosity.

Tom LaBounty cut quite a swath in those olden times. He had ridden with Ben Thompson when the both of them were still colts--before Dapper Ben became a famous shootist. They were both hotheads then, full of themselves, not at all interested in the public conventions. But unlike Thompson, who spent most of his years facing a badge, the legendary Tom LaBounty got hold of himself and wore a star for the next forty-five years. It had taken old-age carelessness and a back-shooting petty thief to finally do him in.

Joe LaBounty lowered the letter. Beyond the car window and his own gray reflection, telegraph poles darted by with a steady *whip-whip-whip*. The clickety-clackety of steel carriage wheels rolling over steel rail joints produced a soothing rhythm, the regularity reassuring. In LaBounty's world, reassurance was currently a mighty scarce commodity. There were precious few moments when his mind was not filled with the terrible images, the awful agony, that for the past year had haunted his every waking moment.

Without really thinking on it, Joe had brought the letter back up. Moving back to the reservation agreed with her, Mary said, living in the country she was raised. She and another woman earned over thirty dollars ricing in early September, parching another fifty pounds for themselves. It was her first time ricing since she was a girl. Mary poled while the other lady flailed the ripe rice into the canoe. The woman practiced the old ways that Mary had forgot, carefully allowing some of the rice to fall back in the water and sink into the muck as seed for the following season.

Pike netting was good too. The men were smoking great

slabs of the juicy fish for winter. The fall berries weren't so many, but big and tasty. The gardens were harvested and the canning done. A little corn was still standing in hopes of some roasting ears before the snow flew. Generally, the band was content. The winter would lack hunger, which had not always been the case in years past. The only thing to worry a body, so she wrote, was a run of Scarlet Fever among the white settlers along the Prairie River rapids.

Joe learned later his mother had gone up to doctor them, despite the fact she wasn't fit herself. No one spoke to her, nobody came by asking for help. No call for it. She had heard of the settler's need and that was that. Joe's mother pulled four little ones through before she took the fever herself. After a week of burning up and not able to properly breathe, what with all the swelling and inflammation in her throat, her great heart gave out. That was the end of Mary LaBounty and Joe was coming home to bury her in the ancient grounds on the shores of Sandy Lake.

Mary LaBounty was a grandniece of Chief Hole-In-The-Day, The Younger. The Mississippi Ojibway had long honored Hole-In-The-Day as a great leader, a man who fought fiercely to keep the whites from swallowing up his people. He worked tirelessly for tribal housing and more reservation land, providing many personal needs for his people. And, while he may have taken more for himself than was proper, his long struggle against the whites and their unjust ways earned him a special place in the hearts of the Chippewas. When Mary returned to the reservation, she reclaimed her heritage from that great line.

She affirmed to dedicate the rest of her life to the good of all people. She had wished only to serve, she said, to help others, to clutch to her own bosom the burdens of anyone in need. She took only enough food to live from day to day and had but one change of clothes. All other earthly possessions were renounced or given away. The band and most of the white settlers around Sandy Lake treated her like a holy woman.

Joe pinched his eyes closed with thumb and forefinger. There had been another reason for her good deeds and saintly ways, one he understood as no one else. While Mary LaBounty's service and generosity came honestly from what was in her heart, she desperately wanted to erase the ghastly stain her youngest son had left upon the family name.

12:15 P.M.
In A Barn South Of Lawler

Krieg Dabek darted through a little-used side door and clambered up the loft ladder dragging a half-filled gunny sack. He tossed it to one side and hastily burrowed a cave in the baled hay. Using stray boards, Dabek trussed up his hidey-hole and, sack in hand, scrambled in on all fours.

He was quite pleased with himself. That dumb deputy sheriff had let him go into the court house shit room alone and all he had to do was quick jump out an open window. It had been a good fifteen-foot drop, but he landed right and didn't hurt anything. Dabek ran straight for the tracks and just like that a freight came by. It was so easy. Hah! And they called *him* stupid!

The train men switched off the car he was on at the N.P. siding at McGregor. He snuck over to the Soo Line and waited for another freight. He was lucky again, but the car got a "hot box," an overheated condition caused by friction on a wheel bearing. At Lawler, they dropped it, and him, off. Dabek got out of town fast and slipped into the woods. He wanted to make sure nobody saw he was in that part of the country. He stayed in the bush for a night, a day, and another night to allow his trail to thoroughly cool.

Today he came across this farm and made for the barn. He needed to rest, figure out what to do next. Along the way, he'd helped himself to some grub, a shirt and coat, and some other useful items. It was these things that filled his sack, or turkey, as he would think of it from now on. He was reasonably certain by the way he had taken the stuff that no one would notice it missing for awhile. Krieg Dabek was pretty good at that sort of thing.

He was also pretty good at being naturally mean, without having to work at it, in the way regular folks might breathe or eat. His appearance matched his disposition. He had an ox's jaw, a flat nose, and little ferret eyes that constantly darted to and fro. His thick hair stuck straight out, like a ball of spikes. Though custom would have considered him clean-shaven, he was neither. Children instinctively avoided him, as did dogs. It was the grownups, consumed by their own agendas and distractions, that consistently underestimated his capacity for malice.

12:25 P.M.
On The N.P. Nearing Aitkin

LaBounty was seized by a headache, the usual side effect whenever he had Mary's letter in hand. He had to get a grip on himself and figure out what he was going to do about matters when he got back to Fargo. Talk had been heavy the other deputies were going to make sure he got the boot, force him out of the department. Joe couldn't abide that, for there wasn't any question but that no one else would give him any police work.

It had been a near thing getting the Fargo job in the first place. A senior deputy that ran the county jail considered himself obligated to Marshall Tom for once saving his life. The fellow owed that he would set things right and saw to it that Joe got hired as a jailer. Unfortunately, the old boy was retired early, probably on account of Joe LaBounty's new boss gave Joe to understand he was on a powerful short leash and could expect no favor, no looking the other way on anything at all, for none would be coming, certain. Joe worked like a galley slave seven days a week, volunteered for every dirty job with never a complaint, but it was of no use--every police officer in Fargo openly despised him.

As the train leaned around a curve, a scruffy lad entered Joe's car and careened down the aisle singing out, "Chocolate, apples, hard candy! Raisins, cheese, crackers!" LaBounty hailed the train butch over and bought an oversized red apple and a couple of boxes of raisins. He polished the apple on his shirt and took a huge, noisy bite. Joe could go for days without eating, then all of a sudden get so hungry he ate like a trencherman.

There was yet another matter he was going to have to face up to. What if Kaymaki came to Mary's funeral? His mother had been very close to Kaymaki and she had doted on Mary. Joe bit off a last bite from the apple and pitched the core in a spittoon. Part of him hoped she would be there, the rest was terrified of the idea.

Kaymaki. What a wonderment.

She had picked up the moniker during her tomboy years, and it had stuck. Her real name was such a queer jawbreaker, so comical when he first heard her speak the words, he had laughed out loud. Joe never tired of hearing her say it, the sounds rolling off her Finnish-accented tongue in that delightful, sing-song lilt.

Kaisa Mariana Matalamaki.

Joe leaned back and closed his eyes, his mind turning the name over and over like an Edison phonograph machine.

Kah-eh-sah Mah-ree-anna Mah-tah-lah-mack-key.

Joe's inner smile faded as he remembered looking into her flashing, powder-blue eyes while she accused him of a deed so heinous he could not bear to hear it. It was the last time they had spoken to one another.

The Northern Pacific passenger train rumbled over a small

trestle and past a gang of overalled men pressing marsh hay. The protracted dry spell had long since taken care of the meadows, and folks, hard up for fodder, were turning to the dried-out swamps. The engineer whistled a long greeting and the farmers waved back. The men passed from Joe's view in a blink, as if a landscape painter had snatched away the canvas. Something like how Joe's life had been ripped from him.

Two years earlier--a lifetime ago to Joe LaBounty--he had been appointed Constable of Balsam, Minnesota. It was a rough, out-of-control lumber town and they had been running through policemen like rainwater through a washboard. His first day on the job, he closed the saloons. Aitkin County had been voted dry some time earlier, but up till then no one in Balsam had enough gumption to enforce the law.

There were a lot of angry lumberjacks milling around the Constable's office that night. Their mood turned even uglier after a liquid recess. When the hoo-rahing finally quieted down, Joe strode out of his office cradling a ten-gauge scattergun. Never said a word, just stared at the boys, all the while stone-still. The whites of his eyes shone out in the black like a mountain panther, so some later said. Nobody could recollect how long the standoff lasted, but it was generally agreed it was the 'jacks that gave up the siege and went on home. Next day, Joe shuttered the brothels. Again, there was grumbling, but LaBounty ended it quickly. In a practical concession, he chose to remain ignorant of one popular sporting house nestled in the woods just outside of town.

That first summer, there had been a pistol "fight." A number of river pigs, men who drove logs downriver to the sawmills, came to town anxious to be relieved of their money. After giving their bottles of John Barleycorn a sound thrashing and tiring of fighting with one another, they began a campaign to tip over the town biffys. They were so far gone and so surprised to find real John Law in town, LaBounty had not found it necessary to do more than fire a few shots in the air, though a few rounds were close enough for some of the boys to claim they heard lead whistle. The privies were saved, and that was the end of gunplay in Balsam. A year later, county leaders were urging Joe to run for Sheriff. After many years of itinerant lawing, moving from one dusty prairie town to another and living in what seemed like the same flea-bag hotel in each of them, Joe LaBounty had come home. And found a home. Even better, he would soon wed the radiant Kaymaki and she would forever be at his side.

Then the unthinkable. Like a flash fire through a dry forest, what was alive and precious moments before was now ashes. Everything Joe had worked for, all that he had dreamt of, was gone. Days passed into weeks, then months. At one point he turned up in a Dakota town he never bothered to learn the name of. It was there that he had his closest brush with what his mother called the greatest evil ever visited upon the red man.

Tom and Mary had been fanatical about liquor, knowing full well the vulnerability of their three mixed-blood sons. The boys grew up with a temperance canon so formidable it would have been inconceivable for them to ever use the stuff. Their training was so rigorous, the indoctrination against ingesting poisonous substances so complete, it extended to chewing tobacco, cigars, and rolled smokes as well. Only the ritual use of kinnikinnick, a mixture of willow bark shavings and tobacco smoked in the red pipestone, was tolerated.

But on this particular rainy Dakota night, shivering beneath a boardwalk under a smelly wet blanket, his body racked with pain because he had been sleeping out and not taking care of himself, all that was past. LaBounty had the seal broke on a whiskey bottle, purchased with the last of his hard cash, and was about to take a pull. The inner hurt had become too great, had grown to beyond anything endurable. He was an empty shell, a subhuman creature cringing in the dusty shadows.

The bottle came up to Joe's lips. He did understand, with what little reasoning was still left him, that when he drank from it that would be the end of him. His Spirit would depart, seek another, more worthy human being to dwell in. Once the brown liquid washed down his throat, never again could he move among his people and call himself Warrior, Protector of the People, Avenger of Wrongs, Provider of Life. By taking the white man's poison, he was forfeit, in betrayal of everything he stood for, all that he had done with his life. He would become nothing--lower than an animal, lower than a worm, lower even than a grain of sand.

But what did it matter? His life was over. All the white men were doing now was piling on the agony. By using the water fired by the underworld spirits he could at least rid himself of the pain, all the many different kinds of physical, mental, and emotional pain. Or so he wanted to believe. Joe LaBounty brought the bottle up to his lips, hands shaking.

A fight started on the boardwalk above him, a two-man brawl fueled by whiskey. One of the men fell to the boardwalk with a suddenness and force that startled Joe, and he lost his grip on the bottle. It dropped only a few inches but, unimaginably, struck a rock. Joe could not believe that stone had been there, in that almost pure bed of petrified dust/sand, a foreign object as unexpected as a tree in the middle of the prairie. The bottle soundlessly collapsed, rather than breaking, and the contents seeped into the silt. For the first time since he was a child, Joe LaBounty cried himself to sleep.

Even months later, when he had finally pulled himself together to some degree, life was barely tolerable. On the worst nights, in bed in his squalid Fargo hotel room at three o'clock in the morning, Joe would reach for his revolver and rub the point of the barrel against his cheek. His gun was an old friend, a loyal comrade that had never failed him. Joe would hold it as a child might clutch a teddy bear, the cool steel comforting against his skin. His eyes would close and he would rub the barrel lengthwise with his hand, in a kind of caress. As the night strengthened, as fatigue enveloped his body, his hold on the gun would slowly loosen. Then sleep, blessed unconsciousness, would come for an hour or two. Someday, he knew, there would come a night when the last drop of hope would whirl down the drain. When he had used himself up, when he could no longer go on. It was good to know that on that night, his loyal and good friend would end the pain forever.

A child on the other side of the coach screeched. The mother slapped the boy and gave him a loud dressing-down. Joe looked out the car window, away from the rude scene, away from the hurt. They were going around a curve and he could see the entire train ahead of him. Enormous clouds of coal smoke were spewing from the locomotive smokestack and rolling over the backs of the cars. It had grown stuffy in the carriage because most of the windows were closed on account of the foul stuff would have been sucked in.

The locomotive whistled as it approached a crossing. There were two longs, a short, and one very long that held until the engine had passed the gravel road. The usual crowd of settlers had turned out to make sure it came and went all right. The men reverently held their hats; the women on the wagons were perched like setting hens, their children waving with open-mouthed glee. The train thundered past them at sixty miles an hour and raced into a tamarack swamp.

Unlike the cedar, spruce, and balsam, the tamarack was a larch, an outlaw tree masquerading as a conifer. While the evergreens always looked like Christmas trees, tamarack needles turned brown in the fall and fell off when the cold came. A larch swamp faced the short days and long nights naked, looking for all the world like a dead forest. As the train sped east, Joe LaBounty felt like a tamarack tree in winter.

12:30 P.M.
Balsam Public School #52

Kaymaki walked out on the porch where Helga Andersen was grimly carrying out her sentence. The little girl had the clean erasers lined up on the wood railing and was clapping together the last two, raising clouds of chalk that got into her nose and mouth and made her sneeze and spit. The girl's long face predictably sagged all the more when teacher came out.

Most of the children had finished their sack lunches and were out playing. Noon Hour--actually only forty-five minutes--was the most fun part of school and there was little time to waste on eating. Or cleaning erasers.

A high-pitched squeal came from the yard and Kaymaki's heart jumped. The children were engaged in a spirited game and one of them had lost control of herself when an older boy loudly commanded: "Pom-pom-pullaway! Come away or I'll pull you away!"

Despite teaching for seven years, she still could not tell the difference between a shriek of terror and a cry of joy. Reminding herself to later check if the child had wet her pants, Kaymaki turned back to the Andersen girl.

"Run along, Helga. A few minutes are left before the bell." The girl broke into a wide smile and bounded down the concrete steps two at a time.

She was sure Helga had been spitballed. Kaymaki had been writing a lesson on the board and her back was to the class. When she turned, Helga was flinging a pencil in retaliation. The Haapoja boy was the likely culprit and Kaymaki determined to keep an eye on him. She dropped the clean erasers in a cloth bag and went inside.

Miss Matalamaki was in a rut. Lately, she had been giving serious thought to leaving Balsam, having come around to the conclusion she had been altogether too long in this little backwater. Her family had emigrated from Finland when she was but twelve years old and Balsam was the only place in America she had ever called home. If she wasn't careful, she told herself, she was going to end up a dried prune.

If not for the fact her ailing folks needed her, or at least made a point of telling her so, she would have gone back to Duluth and tried for a teaching position on the East End, the prettiest part of town. Her only time away from the piney woods had been the two years there attending the State Teachers College.

It had been great fun to live in a real city. There were the Lyceum Theater productions, people-watching in the Spalding Hotel lobby, moving picture show houses, the many motor and trolley cars, department stores, restaurants, the glamour of the shipping port--and yes, she supposed, the social life. There certainly hadn't been much of that for a good long while.

Men had always been attracted to Kaymaki, but she had lately grown more and more indifferent. Since the awful experience with Joe LaBounty, she was more than a little suspicious of them. She instantly thought of Constable Gordie Patterson. He had gotten awful attentive right after Joe left, and it was plain to see he was trying to take advantage of the situation. That had only served to make her even more disgusted with the race. Kaymaki frowned in frustration. At the very least, she had ought to run on down to Duluth and get her a new hat!

She strolled by the desks, stopping behind the big one at the back of the sixth-grade row. Kaymaki remembered it was at that desk that she had first gotten to know Joe LaBounty. When she had first allowed herself to look past the color of his skin and see what an uncommon man he was underneath. She unconsciously stroked the back of the seat.

Kaymaki visualized him walking up to her--that ridiculously tall hat perched atop his head, the ever-present sheepskin coat, his long, graceful stride. She remembered his huge hands, one of which could cover both of hers. There was that rare but breathtaking smile, his lovely berry-brown skin, and that thick mane of bottom-of-the-well-on-a-dark-night black hair. Kaymaki loved to run her hand through his lustrous, sable hair.

It was clumsy at first; many of the townspeople disapproved of their budding relationship. But Kaymaki determined to ignore the slights and looks. She had gotten a taste of prejudice herself as a young girl, a new immigrant who didn't understand a word of English, and hadn't liked it one bit.

They began to see a lot of each other. He was not given to small talk at all, which would have been hard on most ladies. But Kaymaki was a no-nonsense woman and idle talk annoyed her.

She looked instead at a man for his character and commitment. Kaymaki had found Joe LaBounty not wanting on either count; a strangely gentle, but powerful, man who, she believed until the very end, would always be good to her. Until that terrible day she learned the savage in him had risen to the surface.

Tears welled up. Kaymaki's hands jerked off the back of the seat as if she had touched the coal stove.

A boy popped his head through the classroom door. In Finnish, he eagerly asked, "Is it time, Miss Matalamaki?"

"Kyllä, Juho."

John raced for the bell rope and yanked it up and down for all he was worth. Kaymaki composed herself by passing out Free and Treadwell's *Fifth Reader* to every desk. She had determined that this afternoon all the grades would hear/read the thrilling story of *Beowulf, The Anglo-Saxon Hero.*

Kaymaki had still not made up her mind whether she would attend Mary LaBounty's funeral. She wondered if Joe would have the gall to show up and what she would do if he did.

1:05 P.M.
On The N.P. Between Aitkin And McGregor

LaBounty studied the smoke plumes ahead, along the Minneapolis, St. Paul, and Sault Ste. Marie, or Soo Line, where it converged with the N.P. at McGregor. Fall was always bad for fire, but this was the worst he could remember.

For over forty years, countless slash and sawdust piles--what was left of Minnesota's virgin pine forests--had been accumulating along the railroad's right-of-way. The logging companies were supposed to burn the stuff on a regular basis, but weak enforcement and sheer volume had overwhelmed the system. Now, in 1918, under the pressures of the World War, railroaders were increasingly removing the "spark arresters," screens on the locomotive smokestacks, because they reduced the power of the engine. This resulted in small lumps of burning coal being "drafted" out the stack, which set the explosive tinder ablaze. Since Brainerd, Joe had counted five section crews fighting fire.

The car abruptly swayed from side to side, interrupting the regular *clickety-clackety*, when the train rolled over a stretch of rotten sleepers. LaBounty's flat-brimmed, Montana-peaked hat tipped out of the overhead rack and fell into his lap. Kaymaki had never missed a chance to devil Joe about what a queer thing it was. Said it looked the kind only cinema cowboys wore.

Holding the hat made him think of the first time they met. One of the eighth-grade boys--a slow-witted, gangly six-footer--had been caught drilling a peephole in the girl's biffy. Kaymaki thought to teach him a lesson and called Constable LaBounty over to make an "arrest." She was taken by how well he handled the matter and called his attention to a basket social on Saturday night. Joe bashfully joined the bidding, then got surprised when he won her basket. While seated with her in that same gangly six-footer's oversized school desk, all the while fingering the brim of his big hat, he began to fall in love.

Never before had Joe been "social" with a woman of her kind. He called few Europeans friend, even fewer Finns. He and his brothers had always belonged to their mother's world, both in looks and attitudes. Seated at that school desk, Joe became conscious, and then embarrassed, by the way he could not stop looking at Kaymaki. She had classic high cheekbones, a creamy white complexion, and silky, almost transparent, blond hair. Like most young women, she coiled it in large rings atop her head, Gibson Girl fashion. Her only physical flaw, if that was what it was, was a small, turned up nose. When Kaymaki got up to refill their coffee cups, Joe could not help but notice a fine figure undisguised by the standard teacher's uniform--a frilly white, high-necked shirtwaist with bow and a ground-length, navy-blue skirt.

They hit it off so well some of the proprieties weren't observed. One day, Kaymaki became so animated over their conversation, she made an almost scandalous twisting motion with her upper torso. A lady next to them let out a gasping sound and Joe averted his eyes. Another night Joe brought Kaymaki home *alone* in a rented Model T from Cayo's livery. Mr. Matalamaki was quite put out, making it very clear that kind of behavior was out of the question. LaBounty apologized endlessly, and had, so Joe thought at the time, set things right with her father.

Kaymaki also had a habit of somehow taking the lead when it was Joe's place for such. She'd run over to a buckboard and mount up without waiting for him to take her hand. Or ask Joe to dance instead of the other way around. And was forever talking to strange menfolk without being introduced. She even one Saturday went to Ostertag's general store after some school needs wearing a pair of Lee overalls. Such forwardness didn't always sit well with folks, though it never bothered Joe. In fact, most of the time he thought it funny. Where in the world had she ever worked up the nerve to wear a pair of overalls!

The two of them got along in a way that made them both feel they had always known one another. After a few months, there were strong hints that Kaymaki would accept a marriage proposal. Then, the day before his trouble, her father came to Joe's office and demanded that Joe stop seeing Kaymaki. At the time, Joe figured it was the Ojibway burr that Mr. Maki had finally got under his saddle. Her Pa left in a huff and LaBounty let it go at that but was disappointed; he had figured him for a better man.

Joe stood up and put his conk cover back on the carriage hat rack. Odd, it now came to him, how old Mr. Maki had turned cold on him, all of a sudden like. And just on the sunrise side of the blowup too. LaBounty wondered why he had never woke up to that before. Like so much else, the particular incident had got lost in the great storm.

Joe LaBounty never discovered who it was that first told the Great Lie that he had fathered a child out of wedlock, refused to marry the mother, a Mille Lacs Reservation woman, and then abandoned them both to die in a snowstorm. However it happened, the "report" raced through the Balsam community, catching Joe so flat-footed and slack-jawed he did a poor job of defending himself. He could not bring himself to believe the townspeople, folks he had helped and protected, could turn on him so fast. Weeks later, he bitterly realized they never would have done that to a white man. LaBounty had to sneak out of town in the middle of the night, just ahead of a lynch party that made the mistake of first getting itself fortified for the job.

The Northern Pacific conductor came through the door of LaBounty's car and bustled down the aisle, announcing it was "Ten minutes to McGregor." A number of passengers made ready to get off, mostly drummers and loggers on the move. The camps were starting to look for men to go up for the winter cutting. A Negro porter came through offering to brush down the men's suits for a nickel, but nobody took the George up.

Joe made his way to the men's private room. After conducting his business and waiting until he was alone in the adjacent alcove, he took off his coat and readjusted the concealed holster from where it had begun to hitch up. Joe LaBounty carried on his left hip, in a cross-draw butt-forward configuration, a Single Action, Short-Barreled "civilian" Model Colt Peacemaker. It was of standard .45 caliber but with a 4.75 inch barrel, rather than the more conventional, but bulkier, 7.5 inch "cavalry" model. The smaller piece accommodated the need for a less conspicuous sidearm, as the settled society of modern times did not favor having their lawmen running about looking like Wyatt Earp. Joe, and old Tom before him, had also been glad to learn over the many years that the short barrel cleared the holster quicker and cleaner. LaBounty had long been content to give away whatever accuracy the longer gun might have offered.

He patted himself as free of wrinkles as was possible and made his way back to his seat. The slowing locomotive rolled past McGregor's one mile marker and the shrill steam whistle announced their impending arrival. A man next to Joe looked at his pocket watch and said they were right on time. With bells clanging and steam venting, the train lurched to a stop alongside the depot. Joe LaBounty gathered up his grip, put on his hat, and stepped down to the platform.

2:45 P.M.
The Barn South Of Lawler

Dabek dug into his turkey and pulled out a can of baked beans. After prying the lid open with a stolen knife, he greedily shoveled the junk down. He grabbed a slab of raw beef and chewed off a huge chunk. Most needed such food cooked, but Dabek didn't much care one way or the other.

The grub settled him; he'd been pretty hungry. He burped and farted for an exceptionally long period of time, then stretched out. Now he could think, figure out a plan to take care of old lady Prettyman. For what she done, she had to pay.

Mrs. Nathan Dexter Prettyman, widow of the respected Balsam banker, had testified against Dabek at his trial. Mrs. Prettyman told the jury that she had clearly seen Mr. Dabek rape and brutally strangle Krista Jorgenson. It was clear by the nods and body language that the twelve good men believed her; they could barely make themselves even to look at the accused. The court-appointed lawyer whispered to Dabek that her testimony was going to send him to Stillwater State Prison for the rest of his life. That was when he decided he had to make a break for it.

Dabek fondled his crotch and snorted. The old crone didn't have nothing better to do than spy on folks, he thought, spitting out a wad of gristle that had got stuck on a broken tooth. Like everybody else, she wanted to hurt him. Well, he was going to see about that. Now that he was free he aimed to make Mrs. Prettyman pay, shut up her gab hole so she couldn't hurt nobody again. Krieg Dabek decided there wasn't going to be anyone ever gonna hurt him again. No sir. They had always been against him. Even when he was little.

Dabek never knew where he came from. Someone once said his people were from the middle of Europe, but he didn't know nothing about that. He didn't know any of his folks or relations and never cared if he did. He had been shunted from orphanage to orphanage all his childhood. They said he couldn't get along, but he knew it was because they had it in for him. Now and then a foster family would take him in, but they always brought him back to the orphanage. Everybody said he was no account, "anty-social" is what they called it. But they just said that because they wanted to make him suffer. He had figured that out early on.

Once, one of the "foster" women come and took him to her house, but she went and hit him with a pan when he ate one of her pies. It wasn't right to hit him just because he was hungry; she oughten to have done that. A few nights after he got sent back to the orphanage, he snuck over to her place and stuck a pitchfork in her guts. It was the first time he hurt somebody back after they hurt him. It felt good. He had been ten years old.

After the Germans commenced to fighting, Dabek took the name Krieg. An orphanage man had given him some dumb first name when he was little, a name which, he realized a little uneasily, he could no longer remember. Dabek had heard the word krieg when the war started and he liked the way it sounded. He supposed it was a German word, meaning kill or fight or some such. He liked the Germans. They were just like him; when someone tried to hurt them, they hurt back.

Dabek had been on the move all day and, after eating so much on an empty stomach, became sleepy. He decided to get a little shut-eye before figuring out how he was going to kill Mrs. Prettyman. It would need to take some time, so that she might have a good while to be very sorry. He wouldn't have any sport with her though. She was old and ugly. He liked girls young and pretty.

Dabek closed his eyes and dreamily recalled the terrified Jorgenson girl pleading for her life moments before he crushed her throat.

4:00 P.M.
Balsam

Mrs. Nathan Dexter Prettyman bustled up to Constable Gordie Patterson's desk and rapped it hard with her umbrella. "See here, Gordie. What is it you are doing to protect me?"

Patterson clearly didn't like the way she came on, but he struggled to be civil. "Now, now, missus. He won't be back here. Even Dabek isn't that big a fool. Anyways, Sheriff Ike has got the whole countryside out looking for him. They'll catch him, you can be sure."

Mrs. Prettyman wasn't buying. "Fine sounding words, but it wasn't you that testified against him. Oh, if he'd looked at you the way he looked at me in that courtroom, you'd be over in Mrs. Ostertag's blind-pig--don't deny it, I know you go there--sticking your head in one of her jugs and never pulling it out."

Gordie sighed in exasperation. "As God is my witness, ma'am. We aren't going to let anything happen to you. Run along home now and lock the door. Leave things to me."

Annabelle Prettyman could see she was going absolutely nowhere with this. She lifted her skirt and whirled for the door in disgust. "Gordie, you don't know beans. And say what you will about Joe LaBounty," throwing the words over her shoulder, "but I'd rest a good deal easier if it was him sitting in that chair."

Constable Patterson's mouth opened, but Mrs. Prettyman was gone before any sound came out.

4:50 P.M.
The Anker Haakonson Farm North Of Balsam

Ragna Haakonson hooked the rope-handled bucket over the iron pump spout and levered the squeaky handle up and down until the suction caught and water started flowing. "Charlie should not go for cows," she said to her husband. "What if Dabek comes."

"Aw Ma, I ain't afraid of him." Only a few months shy of fifteen, flaxen-haired, nose-freckled Olaf "Charlie" Haakonson stretched himself to his full height. He could fit into his Pa's denim overalls now and figured he was old enough to speak for himself.

"Now Mamma, we can't stop world from turning," Anker

said. "Milking and chores got to be done no matter Dabek come or go. Charlie, shoo."

Mrs. Haakonson bit her lower lip. After wiping her hands dry on her apron, she slipped the two filled buckets onto the carry yoke and trudged back to the house. Charlie was already past the barn, at full gallop, hand clamped on head to keep his cap from flying off.

"Come, Jack!" he yelled as loud as he could. Jack The Dog materialized out of nowhere and came to heel. He was a true mutt, given to Charlie as a puppy by a neighbor who was on his way to drown Jack's siblings. Anker had been skeptical about taking on the mooch, but got surprised when the dog took to cows like hogs to mud. He wasn't a bad bird dog, either.

Charlie clambered over a fence stile and, dodging cow pies in the clover/timothy pasture, made for the woods. He knew about where the stock would be; there was only that little open meadow left that had any grass left fit to graze. He raced by the creek, which for the first time ever showed a cracked earth bottom instead of water. His shoes ground the oak, ash, basswood and maple leaves into powder when he dashed over them.

"G'Boss!" Charlie yelled over and over. "Come G'Boss!" There was the faint tinkle of a cowbell and Charlie signaled Jack to make a big circle toward the sound. The Guernsey appeared out of the brush first, as Bess always did, with the several Brown Swiss compliantly following her. After Jack bunched them up, Charlie took point and slowly led the herd back to the barn.

A couple of minutes later Bess suddenly stopped, her tail switching, curious over a woodchuck that was peering back at her from a hollow log. Charlie yelled at her to get going but she wouldn't budge. Finally, Jack had to nip at her hoof.

She bawled in anger, but finally got back underway. Bess was a cantankerous old bossy; Charlie had come to grief over her many a time. He would have made steaks out of her long ago but his ma insisted on keeping the old thing because her milk was so sweet. It was only recently that Charlie had got big enough to take the job of milking her away from his father, a bittersweet triumph.

All things said, though, he did have to concede her milk was the best he ever drank. His two younger sisters guzzled the stuff by the gallon. It was only the Brown Swiss milk that got loaded in cans and, four days a week, drove to the Balsam Creamery. They took the cream out in their big separator and gave the skim milk back to his Pa, who slopped the hogs with it. Or rather Charlie did. His Pa claimed the work, but it was his sweat... or so Charlie saw it.

The boy opened the barnyard gate and Jack barked the cows through. All day he had been daydreaming about what he would do if the outlaw Krieg Dabek showed up. Charlie had only read about such men in dime novels. He had conjured himself up a notion by which he would sneak up on the bad man, get the drop on him with his .22 rifle, and bring him in irons to Constable Patterson. Oh Boy, would he be somebody! Then he could do what he wanted and not what his dumb old folks made him do.

Charlie Haakonson had been born Olaf, but he never let anybody call him that. He hated the sound of it; it was a Norwegian name, a foreign name. He was embarrassed by his folks because they talked and acted like foreigners. He had lost count of all the fights at school with boys that called him a dumb foreigner. Charlie hated school. He hated farming. He hated his folks. He hated Balsam. It wasn't fair.

Someday he was going to run away and never come back.

6:00 P.M.
The Ojibway Village On Sandy Lake
The Headman sat down for supper and motioned for Joe

LaBounty to do the same. Three other priests of the Midewin, or Grand Medicine Society, joined them, along with a number of other band leaders.

Joe had been gratified to learn he was still considered a Warrior, a member of a very small, extremely secret group of men within the Sandy Lake Band. Judging by the demeanor of the two that were present--the other eight men in the log house were oblivious to any of it--they had likely not heard of his troubles or didn't believe the stories. Joe made a point of making eye contact with each man but he was really only watching the two who, like him, had sworn to combat the white man in his determination to extinguish the Ojibway language and way of life.

The formation of the Warriors was a last resort; even they sometimes could not believe it had come to that. But the reality was inescapable; within the families surrounding them now, parents were not allowing their children to speak Chippewa. It still staggered Joe--forbidding the children to speak the words of their ancestors! The government had told the Indians they could not become real Americans, could never hope to apply for citizenship, without first renouncing the old ways and learning to become white. It was altogether too much for men like Joe LaBounty.

The Warriors had but three rules: No one must ever know they exist, to enter the brotherhood every man must have struck the enemy at least once, and each must be prepared to lay down his life for the good of the band. The selection of an enemy was extremely rigorous, and over the many years only a few had been found guilty. These were unscrupulous whites; men who took delight in ruthlessly stamping out Ojibway heritage, men who killed Indians for fun, men who considered the red man essentially an upright-walking animal. To Joe, it was not so much a battle of races as it was a species war.

Still, it took a matter of the most heinous nature to become a Warrior target; only the very worst, or very dangerous white men, were ever considered. But when they were condemned, when it had been decided, the matter was done. In the old way. Without hesitation. Without pity. Without remorse. Except for his brother Jack, no one Warrior had counted coup more times than Joe LaBounty.

The Headman's wife served a venison and wild rice dish, then slipped away to a cabin next door to join the other women. The men spoke in Otchipwemowin, the Chippewa language. Joe hadn't talked the lingo since he was run out of Balsam and he was having a little trouble keeping up with it.

"It will be as you ask," said the Headman, passing the large plate. "Your mother will receive full rites and be buried here in the holy ground."

"Thank you," Joe said.

"Thornton, the white Priest from Balsam, wanted her. He was going to give a Mass and put her body in the white cemetery next to his church. If you had not come, I would have given her to him."

Joe's raised his eyebrows in surprise. He made no truck with Christians, especially that one.

The Headman continued. "Your mother became fond of the Catholic way. She prayed much to their Spirits. Talked to their Mother. Did the cross over her heart."

Joe grunted. "She changed. That was not her way."

The Headman nodded. "The whites want us to become like them. Wear their clothes, learn their trades, speak their tongue, accept their angry god." He shook his head very slowly. "It is hard to understand a god who does not like what he makes. Why does he not fix the mistake?"

The Headman ladled more food on Joe's plate. "Mary tried to believe, went every Sunday to their church. They liked her; she talked white good. They let her doctor their sick people. She was a good medicine woman. It helped that her husband was white and she had lived a long time among them."

The Headman cleared his throat and drank some coffee. He seldom spoke this much at one time.

Joe made a show of digging into the venison dish. He wanted to change the subject, for he was suddenly and acutely aware of his French blood. He hated that part of him, and the great wedge it placed within him. Ironically, that particular circumstance had made it easier for him to become a U.S. citizen; for only "civilized persons of mixed white and Indian blood" were permitted to apply and generally accepted as citizens. Without the citizenship paper, Joe LaBounty would never have been able to become a professional lawman and follow in his father's footsteps.

"Tell me of the ceremony," Joe said. "How will it go in the morning? That is, what is it I am to do?"

The Midewin priests looked at one another in bewilderment.

After a long moment, Joe set his plate down and bowed his head, ashamed of the lapse. "I sometimes forget the old ways."

The Headman spoke into his plate. "You smell like a white man." He took another spoonful and chewed it mechanically. "You have been away from the Human Beings too long."

2:15 A.M., Friday, October 11th, 1918
The Barn South Of Lawler

Through a crack in the loft floor planks, Krieg Dabek had watched the farmer do his evening milking. The dairyman was a "night" milker; that is, a fellow who milked later in the evening so that he would not have to get up at 4:30 A.M. to do morning chores. It was apparent his children were gone and he felt not the need anymore to put a strain on his system.

Dabek had to be ready to hide when the graybeard came up to fork down hay for the night feeding. If spotted, Dabek would have to kill him. That was bad, would spoil his plans, and so he remained very alert, hiding in the dark shadows.

As it turned out, there had been little to worry about. The farmer worked by feel in the dark loft, guided by decades of operating in the same small space, and hardly strayed more than a few feet from the mow trap-door. He finished his hay-pitching chores quickly and scuttled down the mow ladder. At length, a supper triangle rang out up at the house. Not coincidentally, the farmer was in the act of blowing out his kerosene lamps. Moments later, the barn door latch fell.

During the rest of the evening, Dabek continued his preparations. Around midnight, his eyesight having adjusted to what most would consider pitch blackness, he stepped down the ladder in pursuit of a bale hook. This farm tool was designed for the benign purpose of carrying hay, but had all the appearance of a medieval torture instrument. He selected the strongest looking specimen from an array of five hung on a wall, then scurried back to his den. For the next hour, he carefully sharpened the hook's point with one of the farmer's files.

At one point, Dabek gripped the file so hard his right biceps flexed, tearing his shirt sleeve. That sort of thing had happened so often he no longer paid it any mind. Once he and Butch Phillips, a local strongman, were loading railroad ties into boxcars at McGregor. Butch thought to impress the other men by stacking two tamarack railroad ties over one shoulder at the same time, a weight of over five-hundred and fifty pounds. Krieg Dabek sneered, loaded up two himself, then ordered a couple of men to throw on a third for good measure. He then proceeded to run up the car loading ramp, to the utter amazement of the entire tie yard.

Dabek snacked and dozed in the loft for a long spell before suddenly snapping alert. He was like an animal in knowing when it was time. Dabek had never carried a watch or owned a clock. In his mind, it was one more example of how he was better than other people, how he did not need things like regular folks.

Not that he didn't favor comfortable places to live, good food to eat, girls to make sport with, people to beat up on that needed it. He was like everyone that way, he supposed. It was just that most of the time it didn't matter what he ate or where he slept, or that he might generally have to do without. Silly things like clocks were for stupid people who weren't smart enough to figure the like out for themselves. What Krieg Dabek could never bring himself to admit was that the real reason he hated and avoided clocks was because he had never learned how to tell time.

Now ready to go, he painstakingly restored his hay "cave" to its natural state and put the boards, file, and some other things he had used back exactly as they had been. For safety, he stuck a cork he found in the farmer's trash barrel on the point of the razor-sharp bale hook. He was very pleased with himself for having found another hook in the loft and replacing the one he took.

Dabek wrapped up the crow he had caught and killed earlier, placing it, a few possibles, and the bale hook in his turkey. He threw the bundle over his shoulder and stepped down the haymow ladder. If he walked fast he could be at old biddy Prettyman's about an hour before daybreak. Krieg Dabek knew that human reactions were slowest then.

5:15 A.M.
Haakonson Farm

Bess stepped on Charlie's left foot and he punched her on the flank. The animal shifted her bulk in retaliation, knocking Charlie off the one-legged stool. The milk pail went flying, very nearly knocking over the kerosene lantern.

"You stupid cow!"

Charlie jumped to his feet and with both hands slapped the manure dust from off his butt as fast as he could, as if any delay would increase the possibility of contamination. Fortunately, from the milking standpoint, he had only just started and there had been less than an inch at the bottom of the bucket. The close call with the lantern was another matter and it made the hair on the back of his neck stand on end. There was nothing more dangerous in a barn than a lit kerosene lantern. He swore an oath never to mention the incident to his Pa.

His anger spent, Charlie flipped the stool under his rear and pinched the tin pail between his knees, squeeze-tugging the two largest teats. Twin streams of raw milk tattooed the side of the pail. After a few minutes of hard milking, the bucket was half full and the rhythmic tapping softened.

There was movement over by the grain bunker. Charlie stopped to size things up, thinking it might be a rat. Then it came to him. After nearly a week, old Cat had decided to come on home. Charlie had commenced to wonder if a fox or coyote had got him.

Charlie Haakonson had missed his little contests with that scrawny son-of-a-weasel. Their running fight had developed into something like that trench war going on in France. One side would jab, the other dodge--then they'd trade places. There would be times of cease-fire. Then suddenly, one or the other would launch a sneak attack after having lulled the other to sleep.

Until a month ago, it had been a pretty satisfying scrap. 'Twas then that Cat figured out he was under no obligation to first do battle with Charlie before the boy would fill his milk tin. Unlike many farmers, Anker Haakonson believed a well fed cat made a better mouser. Cat would get his dinner whether he went through any of the fuss or not. The old thing had been ignoring the boy ever since.

Charlie affected an air of nonchalance, pretending he did not know Cat was there. The black and white barn tabby yawned, then moved into the light toward his pie-tin. Yep, he's gettin' careless, Charlie thought, watching Cat all the while from the corner of his eye. All he's thinking about is his dinner. Of a sudden, the cow next to Bess caught her bell in the stanchion and set off a ruckus. Cat started and looked at the cow. Charlie looked back at Cat. Now!

The boy simultaneously dropped his left leg and twisted a teat to near horizontal. After taking quick aim, he let loose a long, continuous stream of milk that caught Cat directly on the puss. The animal leaped into the air screeching and bolted into the darkness.

Charlie laughed so hard he got a side ache. Anker came directly over from the calf pens with fire in his eyes.

"Boy, stop this foolishness! Leave Cat alone and see to milking."

Charlie stopped laughing in mid-guffaw; the way he bit it off almost hurt. He pressed his forehead against Bess' side and milked furiously. His father had always to spoil the fun. The old man didn't care about nothing except making sure Charlie did all the work. Damn, but he hated it here. Damn! Damn! It felt good to swear, even if he couldn't do it out loud. But daggone, things were powerful hard to take!

When he turned sixteen, Charlie Haakonson told himself, he was gonna quit school and run away. He wondered how he would stand the wait.

7:55 A.M.
North Shore Of Sandy Lake At The Ojibway Village

Joe had been sitting on a log near the beach since before dawn. It was a long time ago since he had sat next to the lake, alone with his thoughts. The meditation had somehow calmed him, made him feel a little better about his condition, though nothing had changed.

Just now, he had been noticing signs of fall losing its grip to winter. Great V's of chortling geese and ducks were floating southward down the Mississippi River Valley flyway. The leaves of the shoreline trees were an artist's palette--green pines mixed with red and brown maples, accompanied by splashes of yellow oak. The nights had now grown cool enough to smother the mosquitoes and gnats, though a few listless black flies continued to buzz about harmlessly. The forest to his back was dead quiet save for the hushed pitter-patter of floating dead leaves. To Joe, whose world had lately turned to a barren black and white, it was a morning of unaccountable peacefulness and stunning beauty.

The crazy-woman scream of a low flying loon reverberated across Bill Horn Bay. The ancient bird flew directly in front of Joe, but instead of continuing to follow its flight, his eyes locked on the new columns of smoke to the southwest. Every day now seemed to bring another grass or brush fire. He wondered what it was going to lead to.

The wind was blowing the smoke to the southeast and the

air at Sandy still smelled clean and pure, though it was uncommonly dry. Joe thought the gusts were even stronger than yesterday. Around the lake there was a dark mark two feet above the present water line, confirming the fact Libby Dam had been opened to the Mississippi River. On account of the dry spell, there was a great need for water down below and, as some put it, the U.S. Corps of Engineers had gone and pulled the bathtub plug.

The government did not very much care what would happen to the fishing and the rice beds when they did things like that. Moreover, the bureaucrats couldn't get it into their thick heads that it was the fluctuation of water levels that was bad; if they either left it always high, or always low, like it had been before the dam, it would be O.K. But the way it was done now was the worst. Up and down, down and up--so that not even the fish could tell which way the elevator was running. All that mattered was the loud white voices downstream, bellowing for more or less water.

Joe shook his head to clear it. With all he had on his plate, he could not be worrying himself over things that did not directly concern him. Once the funeral was over, he had to leave this place, get back to Fargo and protect what little interest he still had in this old world. Find a way to make a life, as pitiful as it was turning out to be.

He looked down at his mourning suit, ran his hands over the fine old deerskin outfit that had once been his best clothes. He thought it was a bit of a wonder it still fit, not realizing his indifferent eating habits and physically rigorous work had kept him quite trim. Joe had forgotten how pleasing the suit was, like the way white folks felt, he supposed, when decked out in their Sunday go-to-meeting clothes. Long ago, Tom LaBounty had showed his sons how to waterproof and preserve deerskin by blackening them in a smokehouse. Joe's had been made fifteen years earlier, as had his brothers'. He had not given the suits a thought in ages, but, all along, Mary had carefully looked after them.

His had just the right amount of rawhide frills; the matched colored beads were carefully composed to complement the leather. After so long together, the different materials had given up their individuality and the costume had metamorphosed into a unified work. His older brothers, Jack and Jim, would be wearing similar but strikingly different looking outfits, for the three had been created to match not just their size, but each man's personality. Joe's buckskin had the most symmetry, Jim's the most color, Jack's was the most enigmatic.

His brothers had arrived in the middle of the night; Joe nearly stumbled over them while on a nature call. Both had been sleeping with their backs against a huge pine, nestled in a thick bed of brown needles. You could not tell they were there even if standing next to them. Like ghosts, Joe thought.

Even when they were kids, Jack and Jim had been better Indians than he. They consistently outdid him at hatchet throwing, bow and arrow, canoeing, trailcraft--any of that sort of thing. Tom had once said of Jack that he could follow a month-old woodtick trail over solid rock. Joe's dealings with his brothers had been hard until one day his father discovered the boy's natural ability with firearms. He knew he had found his niche when he overheard his Pa tell a neighbor "my Joe could shoot the balls off a mosquito at a hundred yards."

LaBounty shifted his weight on the log. One leg had gone to sleep. He snorted. It was a pity his brain could not do the same. He had hardly slept last night, his mind relentlessly playing over and over that terrible last scene with Kaymaki. First the screaming and crying, and then the worst--her spitting directly into his face. It had been absolutely the most degrading thing that had every happened to him. Naturally, his tortured, unrested gray matter seized the occasion and had her spitting on him over and over all the livelong night.

LaBounty looked oddly at the willow slip-whistle he'd been whittling on, as if he had just discovered it in his hands and was at a loss to explain what it was doing there. He turned it over a few times. There wasn't enough sap to let the bark slide right. Joe knew before he started they only could be made right in the spring, but he went ahead anyway. He needed something to do with his hands.

It wasn't going to work and Joe flung the stick away. It landed next to a pair of moccasins. With feet in them. Jack LaBounty had emerged from an alder thicket and was standing but ten feet away. Joe stood, bristling, wondering how long his brother had been watching him.

The two hadn't seen each other in five years, but it may as well have been last night at supper for all the demonstration. To someone watching, it would have appeared that nothing at all was going on between them. No speaking, no waving, no running up and shaking hands, no hugging one another. Not even the obligatory forefinger wave. To a stranger, it would have appeared they were not communicating at all.

But strangers wouldn't have seen the nonverbal clues--the locking of the eyes, the subtle body language, how they appeared to one another. It had always been their way, though Jack had taken the 'strong and silent' family trait to a science. Jack LaBounty was the kind of man who didn't waste anything, especially words. In a rare moment of introspection, Joe's oldest brother had once said that only a fool uses up all his kindling on a single fire.

There was, as a matter of fact, little to talk about. Both could see the other was physically healthy. Joe was sure Jack had heard about his troubles, but doubted it would come up. Even if he believed the stories, which Joe considered unlikely, he would consider the matter none of his business. If there had been any other real news, it would have necessitated verbal communication; by its absence there was nothing to report. It followed then, that all was well--and as far as the brothers LaBounty were concerned, the matter was concluded. Without one word having been spoken between them.

Jack LaBounty tossed his head toward a path, which translated as, "It is time to bury our mother," and walked away. Joe got up from the log and followed him down the trail.

The Headman and three priests, along with Joe's brothers, nearly all of the Sandy Lake Band, and a number of Mary's white friends, perhaps eighty people in all, were there. The older Ojibway ladies had blackened their faces, an ancient gesture of deep sorrow. In contrast to their normal everyday appearance, the standard cookie-cutter "white" look that made them supposedly fit in better with the Caucasians, they had plaited their hair and wore traditional dress--blue broadcloth shawls, beaded pantalets, and deerskin moccasins.

Joe barely listened as the chanting began, his eyes fixed on his mother. She had been prepared in the Indian way, simply covered with but a colorful quilt. Joe had vehemently said no to a pine coffin; that was how the whites did it and the idea was intolerable.

Mary LaBounty's body was placed in a sitting position in the grave facing west, the direction of the home after death. At her side was a sampling of her best beadwork and things for the long journey--mosquito netting, pemmican, a bowl of rice, ears of corn, and several everyday items, including a favorite tea kettle. The smaller items filled her makak, a beautifully made birch-bark basket. She wore a conventional white woman's dress--she had no Indian clothes--but on her feet were the beautiful pair of dress moccasins made by her own mother. One of the women wanted to include a crucifix and Bible but Joe forbade it, though he suspected Mary would have wanted them with her.

The Headman nodded at a gnarled old woman. It was

Mary's ricing partner. Without any apparent emotion, she softly sang a long favored Christian hymn in Mary's honor:
"Jesus ish pe ming kah e zhod."
Jesus, my all, to heaven is gone.

Joe LaBounty averted his gaze, so as not to show his disgust, while the woman sang the entire wretched song. He managed to shoot a glance at his brothers for their reaction but they were, as usual, completely inscrutable.

The Headman sat aside his medicine bundle as a signal. The Drum Keeper stopped, and there was silence. Jack and Jim LaBounty approached the grave and presented Mary with a large deerskin pouch of kinnikinnick. They said some things about their mother and her life, then stepped back.

"Ke-go-way-se-kah," the Headman said to Mary. "You are going homeward." With that he walked away. The Drum Keeper started up again and the Midewin priests got to their feet and solemnly danced. And then it was over and everyone left.

Joe LaBounty stayed behind, watching the men close the grave. He stood quietly, very still. An unusually aggressive deer fly buzzed around his face but he ignored it. The only sounds were the thump of dirt clumps hitting Mary's blanket and the cheerful morning song of a red-wing blackbird. On another level, and only for a moment, Joe LaBounty thought he could hear the earth's heart beating.

A shadow loomed over the grave. Joe turned to look from where it came, bringing up a hand to shield his eyes from the sun. Blinking through the glare, he saw a young, black-veiled woman with pale yellow hair. She was dabbing her eyes with a white kerchief. Kaymaki.

8:40 A.M.
Sandy Lake

They sat silently on Joe's beach log. Both looked straight

ahead, across the lake. Above, white cumulus clouds raced across the blue sky, as much in a hurry to be about their business as Joe and Kaymaki were not.

"Thank you for coming," Joe finally said.

She replied formally. "I have my pupils to think of and can only stay a short time but I could not abide myself had I not come. Mary was like a... a very good friend." It was obvious she had almost said mother.

Joe swallowed hard and jumped in with both feet. "It was a lie. I tried to tell you but you would not listen. Will you hear me now?"

Kaymaki flashed her famous eyes, and for a moment Joe thought all was lost. But she composed herself, speaking very deliberately. "I expected you to say something like that. At the least, for your own sake, you ought to own up to the truth."

"I have spoken the truth," Joe said simply.

That was too much for Kaymaki. "Enough! I know what happened. How can you deny that letter from the brother of the woman, from the very brother himself! He was very clear about what had happened to his sister. And when Sheriff Ike hired Gordie Patterson to look into the rumors, he went down there and verified the whole story. Why, Mrs. Wakefield heard the particulars at her boarding table from a Duluth drummer. Even Mrs. Prettyman isn't sure your hands aren't dirty, never mind she has some kind of a soft spot where you're concerned." Her voiced cracked and she had to stop.

Joe felt awful weary. "Their stories all feed on one another, like a snake swallowing its own tail." He made a circling motion with his forefinger. "It is the one that first told the lie that I would like to find."

He had said the last so forcefully, Kaymaki drew back.

"I do not wish to discuss this matter further," she said."Nor will I remain here any longer."

Joe started to speak. Kaymaki raised her hand to him. "No!

I should not have come down to the beach with you."

She stood up and strode back to the village. Joe followed several yards behind. He contrived to arrive at her Reo automobile before she did and opened the door.

Kaymaki hesitated before accepting his assistance. Seated with her hands on the wheel, she looked in his eyes for the first time.

"Go away, Joe. Start over somewhere else, where folks don't know you." A tear came. "I don't ever want to see you again." An Indian boy cranked the motor and she was gone.

Joe was staring at the receding dust cloud when the Headman touched his arm. "The white woman Prettyman uses the talking wire. She calls for you."

Not knowing what else to do, Joe changed back into his working clothes and made for the telephone at the Libby Dam Post Office.

9:50 A.M.
Libby Dam Post Office

"Hello, are you there?" Uncomfortable with a telephone, Joe was shouting into the speaking tube. Having allowed himself to miss breakfast, he was hungry and irritable. Not only that, the dreadful encounter with Kaymaki was still fresh on his mind. The last thing he needed was to be talking into this infernal gadget.

An upset Mrs. Nathan Dexter Prettyman spilled out a story that was nearly incomprehensible. If that wasn't enough, Joe had to hold the earpiece a couple of inches away from his ear on account of a blackboard-like screech on the line. After listening for three or four minutes, he cut in.

"Rein up there, ma'am. If I catch your meaning, you figure Dabek broke into your house early this morning but you didn't see nobody. Then you figured something wasn't right and got to looking around. And you came up with something queer, that about it?"

Mrs. Prettyman cleared her throat and collected herself. "It was a crow. The neck had been nearly twisted off. And its little belly innards were hanging out... Oh, oh, it's Dabek all right. He's leaving me a message. Dead young crow now, dead old crow later..." Joe heard her earpiece hit the floor.

He listened to the scraping as she tried to pick it up. "Sorry, Mr. LaBounty. My hands are shaking something terrible. That awful Dabek..." Joe heard muffled sounds over the line. "And Gordie is no help atall," she came back, her voice an octave higher. "Made light of it when I reported what happened. When it comes to burying your head in the sand, he could give an ostrich a run for its money. I expect he thinks I made the whole business up."

Joe saw where matters were headed. He simply couldn't allow himself to get dragged into this.

"Well, ma'am. Gordie is the law."

"Some law! I'll be dead before he comes to. Look Joe, may I call you Joe?" She didn't wait for an answer. "I'm asking--no... Oh, my word, I'm *begging* for your help! I'll be glad to pay for your time. Whatever you ask. Please, please, Joe LaBounty, you must come to Balsam and help me, for otherwise I will almost surely be killed!"

Joe held a hand over the speaking tube and closed his eyes. Accompanying another of his famous headaches was an image of Mr. Nathan Dexter Prettyman sitting at his big bank desk, talking gently to Joe's folks. Mrs. Prettyman's late husband was loaning a significant amount of money at a very favorable rate to a desperate Tom and Mary LaBounty. His folks had steeled themselves for days to talk Mr. Prettyman down on a current interest rate they could not afford. But all the time--wonder of wonders--it hadn't been necessary. He practically gave the money to them and had not even asked for collateral.

"Everyone needs a line thrown to them at least once," Mr. Prettyman had said cheerfully. While the money was eventually repaid, the LaBountys still considered themselves indebted to the banker. In a way that transcended money. For, as Tom told the boys, what Mr. Prettyman had done made it a Debt of Honor.

Joe took his hand off the mouthpiece. "O.K., ma'am. Sit tight. Wait for me. Don't be worrying about any pay or such. Now, about the-"

"Alfred, is that you? What has happened to my mail?" The strange high-pitched voice overrode even the static on the line, unnerving Joe. It dawned on him he was on a party connection. He wondered how many others had been listening in.

To the new woman, Joe said, "Hold on lady, I'm just finishing up." Then quickly to Mrs. Prettyman, "I'll get there fast as I can."

By the time the party line woman had recovered enough to begin bombarding him with questions, LaBounty had cradled the earpiece. He dropped fifteen cents on the counter, touched his hat in thanks to the postmaster, and walked outside. There were a number of automobiles zipping past Libby in both directions. Shotguns and hunting clothes could be seen behind the side curtains. Sharp-tail grouse hunters, Joe reckoned. Judging from their look, they were well-to-do greenhorns from the Cities. Most were driving heavy cars like the Peerless "Six," autos which were not popular in a region where roads were poorer and scarcer than in the city.

It had been very different when Joe hunted grouse as a youth. In the early years, when the boys were small, Mary had taken them back to Sandy Lake for long stretches at a time. In those days no one worried about particular clothes, fancy guns, or the legal time of year. Results were the mark. He could well remember crawling through the brush, his near-naked body coated black with mud for camouflage and nothing but a rock in each hand. Many hours of considerable discomfort next to a lek, open areas where male sharptails danced for mates and generally hung around, most often went unrewarded. But those times when he took a bird, came home with food for the table earned with nothing more than his wits, brought a profound satisfaction. Joe wondered if he would ever feel that good about himself again.

LaBounty held out his thumb for a time but none of the machines stopped. Finally, a two-seat buckboard emerged from the dust cloud of a touring car and stopped in front of him. An Indian man and woman, he recognized them as Simon and Mary Thompson, sat on the spring seat.

"Going somewheres?" Simon asked. They had been at his mother's funeral.

Joe gestured toward McGregor.

The Indian cocked his head at a very fancy-looking enclosed passenger cabin Marmon 32 speeding by.

"Can't offer as good a ride as that," he said. "But we ought to get there."

"Obliged." Joe jumped into the back and sat down on one of two well-traveled wood crates. He remembered the Thompsons had a couple of kids.

Simon clicked his tongue and the black gelding broke into a trot. At McGregor Joe LaBounty would catch a Soo Line train to Balsam.

10:45 A.M.
Cloquet Union Depot

Northern Pacific Conductor A.K. Easterday deftly placed a pinch of Copenhagen snuff between gum and cheek and said, "I don't like the look of it, Fauley."

Easterday wore a dark blue wool uniform adorned with brass buttons and an official cap with a glass-polished brim that fit perfectly on his head; the whole of it was set off by a dashingly thick gold watch chain strung across his vest. His brush mustache was immaculately groomed, with flecks of gray now in regular appearance alongside the original brown. He looked for all the world, and acted same, like the Captain of an Ocean Ship.

Depot Agent Laurence Fauley was riffling through a stack of papers on his desk. "It's the same on all the roads. Fires everywhere and not the men to put them out. Here, look at this report from the Soo Line." He handed Easterday a penciled letter written on coarse-white, ruled paper.

"A section boss name of Rayno Randa sent it along on a speeder," Fauley said. "He don't write too good, but you get the idea."

Easterday stuck a pince-nez on his nose and read where Fauley had pointed.

"*...had no more than put that fire out when a mile down a nother slash pile commensed to burn from more cole sinders. We run down there, put that out, come back and fond the one we thot out had flarred up and got undergrond into the peet and will likely burn til spring. The wind had come back strong again. I would not set much store in any body telling you we are geting the best of it...*"

"Damn." Easterday tossed the paper on Fauley's desk. "We need more men out there, and right now."

Fauley looked out his bay window, hands on his hips. The design gave him a clear view of the track in either direction. "Like to oblige," he said, "but the road was short men the day the war started and it's only gotten worse." Fauley sat down in his castored chair. "Still, we can't stand around like dopes either. I'll get hold of Stewart and see if he can't rustle up some help." George Stewart was the Great Northern's Superintendent in Superior, Wisconsin.

Both men's heads bobbed at the distant sound of a shrill, almost impatient, steam whistle. Art Easterday stood ramrod straight and tugged on his watch fob, frowning when he looked at it. The eastbound 10:46 was one minute and thirty seconds late.

"Well, by Godfrey, somebody better do something," he said, jamming the watch back in its pocket.

The two men walked out on the platform, with Easterday spitting at and missing a brass spittoon near the door. A bearded man and what appeared to be his two boys were swinging a loaded dray wagon into position. The poorly lubricated cart axles screeched under the load of kegs, sacks, and packages. The older boy had loosened the fastening bolt and was lowering the tailboard. When the train stopped, they would transfer their freight aboard, then receive and deliver whatever goods had been shipped to Cloquet.

Easterday snuffled into the wind. "What about that smoky air, Fauley? You ever smell anything like it before?"

Fauley said nothing, watching the locomotive huff to a stop in front of them.

"It ain't good," Easterday went on, spitting directly on Fauley's platform. "No sirree Bob, it ain't."

Noon
North of Balsam Along The Dead Moose River

Krieg Dabek sat down, fishing in his turkey for food. In his haste to leave Balsam during the night, he had neglected to steal more. There was half a loaf of stale bread left from before, which he wolfed down.

He had gone north into the deep bush after leaving Mrs. Prettyman's. It was rough ground with a good deal of thick undergrowth, hard to traverse in the dark. The alder, birch, and poplar, "weed trees" the old 'jacks called them, were taking over the pine cutover, making it good country to hide out in. He spent the rest of the night under a droopy cedar and got back on the move at first light.

A curious squirrel jumped on the log next to Dabek and twitched its tail, as if it were a dog asking to play a game of fetch. The little critter foolishly moved a little closer. In a lightning-like movement, Dabek whisked the surprised animal from off its perch. A few minutes later, it was roasting over a fire. While his meal cooked, he amused himself by recalling the previous night's events.

After placing the crow on Mrs. Prettyman's chest of drawers, he almost killed her outright. He had been sorely tempted, standing there but ten feet from her bed, listening to the old woman snoring. At one point, Dabek even got out the bale hook and shifted it from hand to hand.

But he stopped himself. It would have been too quick, too unsatisfying. He wanted to throw the fear of the devil into her first, let a real good scare work her over for a day. Besides, he was enjoying how all this was giving him the urge for sport. He could not forget how sexually aroused he had become the longer he taunted the Jorgenson girl. That had reached a climax when she got on her knees, hands clasped together as if in prayer, her eyes leveled at a point just below his belt, and said she would do anything if he would not kill her.

While Dabek did not desire Mrs. Prettyman the way he had the Jorgenson girl, the prospect of time with her still excited him. Krieg Dabek had discovered how powerful good it made him feel to make females beg. He suddenly giggled, like a child anticipating some forbidden delight. His plan was working.

Dabek believed he was good at planning and knowing how things related to one another. He was amazingly skilled with machinery. Whenever petty thievery failed to properly provide for him, he'd take a temporary job as an automobile mechanic. He once took apart a whole car and, without any help at all, put it back together exactly right. He could do the same with gasoline-powered generators, or electric motors, or any kind of mechanical contrivance actually. As long as he could take it apart first. That was the key; if he couldn't take apart a machine first, he had not a clue how it went back together.

Many the time, garagemen offered him permanent jobs. But he never took them, sticking with the on-and-off work. He never liked to be tied down and having to be around people too long. As long as the stealing held out; well, that was a lot easier.

Dabek slipped the squirrel off the branch skewer and ate ravenously. Afterwards, he walked down to the river and drank his fill. Warming his back next to the fire, Krieg Dabek rubbed his hands in anticipation. His imagination was working overtime and another giggle escaped. Oh yes, Mrs. Prettyman was going to get hers! He couldn't hardly wait.

12:10 P.M.
The Beanery In Balsam

"What's the collection for?" Kaymaki asked Mrs. Miller, the proprietor of the eatery attached to Mr. Cayo's livery. There was a huge glass jar on the middle of the counter, already half-filled with coin.

The place was busy and Mrs. Miller had to almost shout over the clatter. "You recall the Claus Blomberg's that moved to Superior?" The gray-haired woman had her head wrapped in a tight hair net and was flipping several particularly greasy hamburgers on the griddle. "I got a letter their boy was killed at the battle of Argonne Forest in France. Mrs. Blomberg wants to visit his grave when the war is over, but has not the means."

Kaymaki remembered Henry, a fine boy with unlimited prospects. He had been one of her favorites. She reached in her wrist bag, drew out a paper dollar, and stuffed it into the glass jar. Mrs. Miller raised an eyebrow at the size of the donation as she sidled over to take Kaymaki's order.

"What'll it be, the feather or the leather?"

Kaymaki had her mind on other things. "I'm sorry?" she said.

Mrs. Miller eyes nearly closed in mirth. "Chicken or beefsteak?" She barked like a seal.

"Never mind," Mrs. Miller said abruptly, holding up her hand. "You want chicken. What beef I got left ain't fit for Krieg Dabek."

Kaymaki finally caught the joke just as Constable Patterson came over from where he'd been playing euchre with some Aitkin men. Gordie had lately been stepping up a campaign to run for Aitkin County Sheriff. Looking important, he plunked his carcass down on the empty stool next to her.

"Well, well. Hello Kaymaki. Taking a break from your little school brats?" He *heh-hehed.*

Kaymaki raised her coffee cup to lip level, steadying it with both hands. She anchored her elbows on the counter. "Why is it, Mr. Patterson, you are not in hot pursuit of Krieg Dabek? Leaving it for someone else to do the dirty work?"

Without waiting for an answer, she set her cup down on the saucer, a little harder then intended. "And if you *must* address me, I expect to be called by my proper name. Now then, let me further say that the seat you are occupying belongs to Miss Kelley, who will be rejoining me momentarily. Good day."

Kaymaki resumed her study of the three-tier glass shelf behind the counter that, after the morning rush, was now only one-third filled with Mrs. Miller's famous raised doughnuts.

Patterson glanced from side to side, mortified at having been dressed down in front of half the town. His new Aitkin friends were having trouble not busting out into open laughter. For a moment, Gordie looked to have a notion to stand up to Kaymaki, but thought better of it. After several clumsy moments, he slipped off the stool and drifted out the door.

With a tight, approving look, Mrs. Miller refilled coffee

cups all round. After pouring Kaymaki's, she leaned over the counter and spoke in a low voice. "Word is this Miss Kelley is going to be our new schoolmistress. Folks are none too happy over the idea of losing you."

A little alarmed, Kaymaki spoke loud enough for all to hear. "But don't you see, Miss Kelley is to be hired as a second teacher as we get ready to go to a graded school. New settlers are coming in every day, and we are long past due for the change. We expect up to sixty-five pupils after the Christmas holiday. I will have the Upper Room, grades 5-8 and Miss Kelley the Lower, grades 1-4. Mrs. Young, the county superintendent of schools, wanted me to look her over."

Matron Miller brightened, picking up the slice of apple pie she had just served Miss Kelley. "This is yesterday's. I'll bring a fresh piece from right out of the oven." Kaymaki smiled at Mrs. Miller's ample backside as the woman bustled away.

The bell on the Beanery door jingled and Miss Kelley walked in, back from freshening up. She immediately got a puzzled look on her face. When she left, folks had their heads down and were going out of their way to pay her no mind. Now, as she walked to her stool, everyone in the cafe was nodding a greeting and smiling brightly at her.

Everyone but Kaymaki. She was staring hard out the front window, her attention riveted on a man wearing a tall hat walking up the street. He stopped and turned in at the walk to the two-story frame house of Mrs. Nathan Dexter Prettyman.

12:20 P.M.
Mrs. Prettyman's Home

Mrs. Prettyman led LaBounty into her sitting room and sat him down on a large rocking chair. It was a high-back New England made piece, solid oak and well over one hundred years old. Between her chair and his rocker was a very large rag rug that bore colorful witness to Mr. and Mrs. Nathan Prettyman's past wardrobe. "Would you like a bite to eat, Joe?"

"Yes, ma'am. I have not had a chance today to give food much thought."

"Understandable," she said. "First you bury your mother, then travel some twenty miles to deal with a hysterical woman in a town that tried to lynch you a year ago. And the day is not half over."

Joe was both amused at her directness and grateful for the opening to talk about something that had been bothering him all morning. "Mrs. Prettyman, about my necktie party." Joe leaned forward and clasped his hands together. "I was wondering if you might be able to freshen up my recollection. I was out of sorts at the time and... Well, I was a particular mess."

Mrs. Prettyman smiled sympathetically.

"Anyways," Joe continued, "maybe you could say why the heat went suddenly off after I left that night. There was no arrest warrant, nobody lit out after me. From where I see it now, everybody up and forgot the whole business once I'd been run off. Powerful odd thing that was, now that I look back on it." He cocked his head. "Don'tcha think?"

Mrs. Prettyman looked very hard at Joe. "I had never thought of it the way you just put it. Something has always bothered me about that whole business, but I never could put a finger on it." The widow lady was standing in front of her green-tiled, mahogany-mantled fireplace, toying with a brass paperweight, when she abruptly took matters in another direction. "I want to apologize for the way I behaved over the 'phone," she said in a new, almost professionally modulated voice. "I had the whim-whams and couldn't think straight."

Joe was irritated. Although it sounded as if Mrs. Prettyman had sympathized with his plight, she had nevertheless changed the subject without really responding to his question. On top of that, there was a new mystery. She wasn't sounding at all like the hysterical woman on the telephone. He had taken with him from his former time at Balsam an image of her as a crank and town busybody, but that was hard to square with the woman that had just spoken. Fact was, Joe knew not a thing about Mrs. Prettyman. Who her people were, where she came from, or how well fixed she was. In all the time before, he had not said but a good morning to her.

Joe's stomach growled loud enough for both of them to hear it. "I was wondering about a little coffee, ma'am?"

"Oh Joe, I'm so sorry! Here I go and make a promise of food to a starving man and promptly go back on my word." She quickly poured a cup from a finely embossed silver urn resting on an oriental wood side table and hurried off to the kitchen.

LaBounty waited until she had disappeared before he got up to look around. Judging from what he saw, he had the answer as to how well off she was. Everything in the house was first class and very expensive. He returned to his chair, shifting uncomfortably. LaBounty wasn't at all certain how much he wanted to know about the woman, or how deep he was willing to get into her affairs. Joe's head flooded with images of Fargo police deputies plotting to get rid of him.

Over cold roast beef sandwiches--Joe ate three of them, along with chocolate cake and more coffee--Mrs. Prettyman told the story of Krista Jorgenson's murder. The old woman had been sitting in the dark, right here in the parlor, something she did a lot, she told Joe, when reflecting on her life with the late Mr. Prettyman. The blackness helped her create more realistic, even colorful, recollections of their life together. Looking out the window that inky night, she watched Krista walking down the boardwalk. Mrs. Prettyman was horrified when she suddenly disappeared into a dark alley. The blink of an eye and the girl was gone. It was not like a young woman to move that way, she told Joe. It looked for all the world like someone had grabbed Krista.

Joe couldn't help pointing out that if Mrs. Prettyman had not been sitting in the dark for a spell beforehand, the pupils in her eyes wouldn't have been dilated enough for her to see a thing that far away. She'd have missed the whole party. When he said same to her, Mrs. Prettyman chuckled ruefully.

Joe leaned backed in the big rocker as she continued. It had been some journey that had brought her to that window. After Mr. Prettyman went on to his reward, she became quite lonely. At length, she discovered that one way to be at least a part of the community was to become the person to talk to if others wanted to know about the comings and goings of the Balsam community. She soon became a regular exchange. Many, she supposed, considered her an old gossip, but that seemed harsh. She was genuinely interested in and wanted to help folks, and the activity filled a vacuum in her emotional life. Strangely, the need to mix in had gotten more acute as time passed and her involvement grew proportionately.

Joe excused himself and got up to get a glass of water, having, once again, neglected himself to an alarming degree. He had not a clue he had become so thirsty and drank three large glassfuls from her kitchen hand pump. Before his troubles, he had always been careful to keep the edge, always attentive to his physical needs so there would be no effect on his judgment or performance. But these last few days in particular, he had become very careless. When a man lacks the vigor for life, it comes to that. Joe pumped a fourth glass and returned to the sitting room.

Mrs. Prettyman took up exactly where she had left off, explaining that she couldn't stand not knowing what had happened. "It was only the day before Krista told me her beau had asked to marry her and she had said yes. She was so full of herself; all she could think about was to get to keeping house.

She said it several times, 'Oh, but I want to get to keeping house.' When I thought about that I threw on a wrap and went out in the night, toward the alley."

Joe blinked a couple of times. The old lady had sand.

"The brute nearly gave me the slip," she said, "but made a mistake when he neglected to put out a lamp in the room where he dragged her."

"Dabek was crazy-drunk, thrashing around and making guttural, unnatural noises. It was as if he had reverted into some kind of beast, as if in his passion his guard had been lowered and his true inner self became exposed." Mrs. Prettyman was sickened at what was happening, at the brutal sexual acts Dabek was performing and forcing to be performed. She made herself watch in order to bear witness, to be ready to help Krista afterward, expecting Dabek to turn the girl loose after he finished with her. Mrs. Prettyman was horrified, and later guilt-ridden, when before her eyes Dabek brutally murdered Krista Jorgenson.

"I should have sounded the alarm right away," she told Joe, tears streaming down her cheek. "Now there is that awful crow." She sagged in her chair and her voice was barely audible. The woman on the Libby telephone had returned.

While a withered Mrs. Prettyman excused herself for a nap, Joe made an inspection of the house. It didn't take long to learn the woman hadn't imagined things; someone had indeed entered the building. He found two separate, although very faint, footprints in the floor dust, one on the basement steps leading to the first floor, another in Mrs. Prettyman's bedroom. The shoe that made them was distinctive and enormous.

Joe carefully examined the dead crow, still on the chest of drawers where Mrs. Prettyman had discovered it. Its grotesque condition and positioning had Dabek written all over it. He noticed none of the windows in the house were locked. Careless, but not unexpected. Joe always puzzled how folks faithfully locked their doors but failed to give a second thought to the windows. Dabek likely slipped in from one in the basement, then made his way to her bedroom. Not surprisingly, she hadn't heard him. The man could move like a panther.

Joe returned to the crow for a closer inspection. The bird had been slashed in a fashion so as to expose all its insides. The knife work--some other cutting tool, Joe wondered?--was meticulous. The guts hung out in a particularly gruesome fashion. The bird's head had nearly been wrung off, hanging on by little more than a shred of skin. Joe scooped up the stinking carcass with a newspaper and took it outside.

He returned to the parlor and paused at the staircase to the second floor bedrooms. Dabek could easily have killed Mrs. Prettyman this morning. But why hadn't he? Was he after bigger game?

Joe mulled it over for a time before concluding that indeed she was the intended victim, and that it was to be no simple, quick death. All this monkeying around was just Dabek's way of complicating the matter up so that it might provide him more amusement.

Folks had laughed when Joe once suggested that Krieg Dabek was smarter than many gave him credit for. He didn't think those folks would laugh now, not if they saw what he had seen. Joe was sure Dabek had everything all planned out, but how to get into that jumbled head of his!

And then the light bulb came on and Joe understood. What he wanted to do was terrorize the woman. Mrs. Prettyman, Dabek had decided, needed ample time to contemplate her grisly fate. It was something like falling off a tall building and knowing all the way down that you were absolutely going to die. Only in Mrs. Prettyman's case, seconds of horror would become hours, perhaps even days.

Rested and with nose freshly powdered, her carriage manifesting a renewed bravado, the widow Prettyman rejoined

Joe in the parlor. Still, she sat down shakily. LaBounty decided the time for handholding was past. She had to do her part in what happened next.

"Mrs. Prettyman, I'll be staying the night."

"Do you think he'll be back, Joe?" She of course knew the answer, but was refusing to deal with it.

Joe was tired of pussyfooting around. "Ma'am, this fellow's first aim is to make you crazy-scared. From the way you look, he's on the right trail." Joe paused for effect. "You can bet your bottom dollar he's coming back. He can't wait."

Mrs. Prettyman stood up from nervousness. Joe continued. "He'll enter this house sometime tonight and sneak up in the dark. He'll wake you in the most startling way and then he'll spend several minutes--an eternity for you--telling you exactly what he is going to do. And then he will proceed to do it.

"He will strip you naked and take his knife, or whatever sharp instrument he is using, and he will cut your arms, breasts, genitals, cut all over your body, and let you feel the terrible pain and watch yourself bleed. He will make you beg for your life, and then laugh in your face. And when you grow very weak"--Joe took a deep breath--"he is going to slash your abdomen wide open. He will smile at you as your entrails fall out on the floor. You will be in excruciating pain, hoping, praying to die. Dabek will watch you carefully, hoping you will last a little longer, suffer horribly just a little more. And then, in that split-moment *before* you die, he will grab your head and rip it from your body."

A slack-jawed Mrs. Nathan Dexter Prettyman swooned into an overstuffed chair.

2:30 P.M.
Three Miles Northwest Of Balsam
Along The Soo Line Track

Section boss Rayno Randa rammed the spade into the peat

and pried up another smoldering chunk. He turned the load over and whacked it several times with the flat side of his shovel. One by one, the glowing embers feeding on the carbon-rich soil winked out. He scattered the pulp to be sure the fire wouldn't spring back to life.

To the northwest were a dozen more wispy, smoke columns. "No end to them," Rayno grumbled, as he tipped back his black kromer cap to let the breeze cool away the perspiration on his forehead.

Smitty, the other section hand, yanked his shovel free of a burning slash pile and shielded his face from the heat. He could barely stand to free the tool; the pine scraps were burning like gasoline. "Won't never catch up without more help. We been farther behind than the caboose since the rest of the boys got sent off to fight Kaiser Bill." Smitty had been too old to be examined for the draft and Rayno was rejected due to the condition of his feet. Rayno Randa had not taken the matter well.

Aggravated with an especially fibrous patch of peat that wouldn't let go of his shovel, Randa unleashed a torrent of obscenities. "Damn the war! Shittin' loggers! Sonofabitchin' railroad!" Rayno could work up a hate that was no little thing and it sometimes blinded him. Without thinking, he tore at the clod with a bare hand, touching an ember.

Randa's shriek exploded across the savanna, echoing off a birch island and flushing a pair of mallards from an unlikely puddle in the desert-like moor. He seized the spade by the end of the handle and flung it as far as he could, missing Smitty's face by inches.

"Good damn you, Randa! Forget that business with Gunnar!"

Rayno boiled over, rushing Smitty. "I'll be choked with a sawlog if I will!"

Smitty spoke evenly. "Don't get cussed with me, Finn boy."

Rayno took a step back, holding his burned hand and grimacing. Smitty might be pushing sixty, but he was still the toughest section hand west of Duluth.

"Ah hell, don't get sore, Smitty," Rayno said. "You'd be riled, too, if your brother nearly got planted."

Smitty went back to work, smacking a glowing ember. "Mebbe. But the way I see it, you got no kick. Eli stuck his nose where it don't belong and Gunnar gave him what for."

"Now that ain't so," Rayno said. "Eli told me for fact Gunnar was trying to cozy up to my girl."

That was too much for the old-timer. "Your girl! Why that there gal come sashaying down the boardwalk, hair a-flappin' under that fancy straw boater, those pearly whites flashing like piano keys--like to blind a man, they would--and danced on up to Gunnar as big as you please. Happy as clams they was, until Eli horned in."

Rayno wasn't listening to his friend. "That maggot-faced, monkey-brained, just-off-the-boat, Swedish son-of-a-bitch took advantage, and when my brother tried to put a stop to it, Gunnar busted him up something terrible."

"Gunnar can't help he's Paul Bunyan," Smitty said.

"Don't give him call to do what he done. I tell you, I'm gonna get that Swede. I'm gonna get him good."

The older man straightened up from his shoveling and faced the younger. "You do that Rayno Randa, it'll be the law. And I'll be with them that come for you."

3:15 P.M.
McGregor Northern Pacific Depot

Train Boss Easterday jumped off his slow-rolling Duluth-to-Staples local and bolted into the agent's office. He tossed the surprised fellow a piece of paper and barked, "Wire Cloquet at once!" Easterday raced back across the platform and swung himself aboard the rear chariot before the telegrapher had even got the message read:

WESTERN UNION TELEGRAM

RECEIVED AT: MCGREGOR 3:17 PM
FRIDAY, OCT 11, 1918
TO: AGENT FAULEY
CLOQUET UNION DEPOT
BIG FIRE BETWEEN TAMARACK AND MCGREGOR EVERYONE OUT PLOWING FIREBREAKS BUT NOT ENOUGH MEN SEND ANY HELP POSSIBLE END
EASTERDAY

4:10 P.M.
One Half Mile South Of The Haakonson Farm

Charlie Haakonson was playing kick-the-rock on his way home from school. The egg-size stone started to make a circle in the gravel road but he made no effort to correct it, just kept kicking it round and round. He was in no hurry. Miss Matalamaki had bawled him out for acting up when he ought to have been doing his sums. It would not have been so serious except he had made the fatal error of sassing her back. In Charlie's pocket was a note to his folks. He would be staying after school all next week.

Pa would be furious. He always was if there was any delay at gettin' to chores. Charlie was convinced his folks didn't care whether he done wrong or not, just as long as there was someone to do work and chores. Of course, they were so dumb they couldn't read the note. It was written in English and they couldn't read nothin' but Norwegian. He would have to read it to them, tying his own noose. And if he fudged and they found out later, he'd be in even hotter water.

Charlie booted the rock into the ditch. A rusty can had caught his eye. He flattened the tin with his heel, then commenced to kick it down the road. Wasn't fair a bit, everybody always picking on him. Charlie kicked the can again, but it didn't want to roll. He spat. Stupid can! It followed the rock into the ditch.

Too soon, Charlie arrived at his lane. He saw the chickens were too far away from the yard again. They liked to come down and peck at the gravel covering the corduroyed township road. Birds are always looking for the right gizzard grit in order to best grind up their food. Charlie ran after them, supposedly to chase the buggers home, but what he really wanted to do was get close enough to boot one of them off the road, too.

"Shoo! chick! chick! chick! shoo!"

The clucks squawked and circled, their little pea brains thoroughly confused by what Charlie wanted them to do. Finally they got the idea and headed for home, with the exception of the old rooster who continued to stand his ground. Charlie picked up a rock and threw it at the cock. The bird reared up and flashed his spurs, then scratched angrily at the gravel.

"You son-of-a-bitch!"

It was only in the last few days that Charlie had dared to swear out loud. So far, he only did it quietly to himself, practicing his hells and damns, using different kinds of voices to figure out which way sounded best. But this was the first time he had said bad words out loud in anger.

Charlie picked up an even bigger rock and heaved it as hard as he could. It would have killed the chicken had it hit. This time the rooster got the message. He retreated slowly, zig-zagging down the lane after the hens, one eye trained on Charlie should the boy decide to launch another attack.

The exchange vented a good deal of Charlie's anger. He decided he ought to get right to chores. Maybe if he did an extra good job today, his folks would be in a better mood when he produced Miss Matalamaki's note.

He eyed the pigs in the pasture, some distance away from where he normally fed them. It was always a trick to get the baskets of corn to the hogs without the critters running you over. He would lay out their feed first, before he did anything else, before they caught on to him.

It was when Charlie clambered up the ladder to the corn crib access door that he first noticed the huge smoke cloud to the north.

4:40 P.M.
Balsam's Potter Hotel

Kaymaki closed the lobby door and unpinned her hat. The jingling from the door bells had faded by the time matron peeked out of her little office.

"They're waiting in the dining room," Mrs. Potter said with a tight smile.

Kaymaki walked through the double doors. Five men were sitting around the table drinking coffee. They were split into two groups. Two men were speaking English to one another; the other three were on the opposite side of the table rapidly conversing in Finnish. Chairs scraped as they all stood for Kaymaki while she seated herself.

The Aitkin County Board Chairman deferred to Fourth District Commissioner C.A. Maddy, who took the floor. "Thanks for stopping by, Kaymaki. It always goes a good deal smoother when it's you doing the translating."

Three-fifths of the Salo Township Board, the other two being English speakers who had already been talked to and had left before Kaymaki arrived, said essentially the same thing to her in Finnish. Then everyone settled down to business. Mrs.

Potter would soon need the table back in order to get ready for her supper boarders.

Mr. Maddy spoke first, with Kaymaki doing the honors. "Gentleman, we have but one subject on the table this afternoon. I am pleased to announce the Aitkin County Board has voted to memorialize their full support of the Balsam School expansion. Your town has grown by leaps and bounds in the last few years. The Board wants to do its part in ensuring the little ones of the Balsam community receive proper schooling.

"Now, I spoke by 'phone to Mrs. Young moments ago and she has approved Miss Kelley as a second teacher." In an aside to Kaymaki, Maddy said, "She seemed most pleased with your report." Kaymaki had telephoned Mrs. Young right after school let out.

Maddy went on. "Rather than wait around till next year, the County Commissioners want to know if you, the Salo Town Board, would be able to accommodate eight grades after the children return from Christmas Vacation. That is to say, get a jump on Eighth Grade accreditation for the 1919-1920 full term."

One of the Board members spoke. "Well, we are not certain what is expected of us. The building addition, yes, it is finished. Now you say Miss Kelley is coming, and that is good. But how to set up the school right, so it is all proper, this is still a question for us."

"Mr. Maddy, if I may?" Kaymaki interjected.

C.A. motioned her to go ahead.

"After I spoke to Mrs. Young this afternoon, I rang up Mrs. Marcus Nelson at Tamarack. She was quite involved when they went to an eighth-grade level school a few years ago. I think you know, Mr. Maddy, Mrs. Nelson has been very active in school affairs in our end of the county. She has offered to meet with me and help us finalize our plans."

"How does that sound to you, gentlemen?" Maddy asked.

The Finns were all smiles. They were more than ready to delegate the responsibility; schooling was an issue they knew little of.

"Hate to always impose on you, young lady," Maddy said to Kaymaki, "but, of course, that is the price a person pays when they are known for getting things done. I think you ought to run up to Tamarack first thing tomorrow morning. Don't let's us have any grass growing under our feet!"

The commissioner loved to turn on the charm even when, as in this case, it wasn't necessary. Kaymaki had a vested interest in getting the new school off to a good start.

But Kaymaki had another matter. "Mrs. Nelson informs me there is a big fire close to Tamarack and does not advise travel up that way right now."

"Oh posh," Maddy said. "I've seen the smoke too. We always have fire around us in the fall. I'm sure they'll have it well in hand by morning." He smiled his politician smile, and that ended it. The men said their goodbyes and filed out of the room.

Kaymaki gathered up her things and walked out to the lobby. Annabelle Prettyman was there, picking up a large dinner basket from Mrs. Potter. Kaymaki walked up to her, thinking the poor old widow lady could use a word or two of encouragement.

Mrs. Prettyman spoke first. "School business?"

Kaymaki almost burst out laughing. As much of a trial the woman was either going through or putting herself through, her investigative instincts remained intact.

"Yes, good news. We are to have a graded school. Balsam children will now have the opportunity to become Eighth Grade graduates."

"I'm glad," Mrs. Prettyman said, without much feeling. Kaymaki glanced at the large basket of food. The woman was obviously expecting someone for supper.

Mrs. Prettyman read her mind. "Joe LaBounty is staying the night at my house." Annabelle's mouth suddenly formed an O and she added hastily, "For protection, don't you see?"

While Mrs. Potter tittered, Kaymaki reassuringly touched the widow's arm and discovered she was trembling.

Mrs. Prettyman glided out of reach. "At least he understands I am in real danger," she said, reflexively dabbing her rouged cheek with a kerchief. "He called Sheriff Ike this afternoon and told him Dabek was in Salo Township."

Kaymaki was surprised. She had heard about Mrs. Prettyman's supposed encounter with Krieg Dabek last night. Like everyone else, Kaymaki thought the whole thing far-fetched. Mrs. Prettyman up to her old tricks, as it were. Now, she wasn't so sure. Whatever Joe might be, he was no fool. He was taking the old woman seriously.

Annabelle Prettyman worked herself up to an announcement. "Joe believes Dabek will try to kill me tonight," she said, defiantly jutting her jaw but unable to control the trembling in her lower lip. Kaymaki and Mrs. Potter looked at each other.

Mrs. Prettyman flabbergasted the other two women by what she said next. "You know, I don't believe he did anything at all to that Mille Lacs woman. If there ever was a woman. You see, I decided to call Sheriff Ike myself this afternoon. It seems that after Joe was run off this brother of hers wouldn't cooperate with the law, Ike thought at the time because he had some dirty linen of his own. They never could get a warrant for Joe's arrest, so the matter was quietly dropped. Now Ike's not sure what to think, for he has heard the brother is now telling a different story altogether." Mrs. Prettyman stroked her dinner basket, then looked directly at Kaymaki. "If I were you, young lady, I'd make it a point to learn the truth about Joe LaBounty."

6:00 P.M.
North Of Balsam Along The Dead Moose River

Krieg Dabek shivered violently. It had been some time since the barking dogs had driven him into the water, and he was feeling it. Although the air temperature was relatively warm for the time of year, the river water was very cold. Dabek understood it was slowly sapping his strength and that he couldn't stand it much longer.

He was crouched under the exposed roots of a scrub oak, with only his shoulders and head above water. He had wedged his turkey into the opening of a fox den in the bank next to him. It was within arm's reach, in case he had to move fast. The muck bottom was very nearly clay and his feet felt like they were under suction. He wondered how hard it was going to be to pull them free.

The dog yapping was getting fainter, moving away to the south. Dabek grunted; they hadn't picked up his scent. They were leaving. Still, he would give them a few more minutes, make dead certain they were gone before getting out of the river. He was very cold but he had not lost his sense of caution.

Suddenly, branches snapped and dead leaves crunched in the underbrush behind him. The voices of several excited men became distinct. Dabek pressed the back of his head against the soft bank, forming an indentation that made him almost invisible from a profile view. He knew instantly what had happened. Part of the posse had stumbled into the opening that had been his camp.

"Look!" cried one of them. "Fish guts!"

"Judas Priest!" another said. "Look at these tracks. Nobody got big, pigeon-toed feet like that 'ceptin Dabek."

"Maybe the dogs spooked him and he's on the run," said still another. "Bet he's heading east, away from the hunt."

The second man chimed back in. "Well, come on. We got him on the run. Can't let the other boys have all the fun!"

"Hold on," said the first voice, obviously the leader. "Let's not lose our heads."

The man lit a candle in the fading light to study the ground--Dabek had keen eyesight and could see the glow against the bark of his scrub oak. The three men were that close to him.

"I don't see any sign to the east atall," said the leader. "Fact is I can't make out much of anything. He'd a left clear sign if he was spooked, being in a hurry."

The leader squatted next to where Dabek had built a small fire. Dabek heard him stir the ashes and could even make out the fellow scratching his chin stubble.

"I don't think he rabbited at all," the leader said. "He's crazy-smart, that one. I'd make book he's gone the other way, to the north, figuring to give us the slip."

He tapped one man on the chest. "Gooz, you go straight across the river here. Me and Billy will swing out around the two sides. We'll meet yonder by that dead pine on the other side." He pointed at a large skeleton of a tree with an eagle nest on top. "Look for any kind of sign-- footprints, broke branches, tramped grass. It's getting dark fast so keep your eyes peeled. Dabek don't leave much to look for when he's on the move."

The two other men disappeared into the brush while Gooz Gustafson hurried forward. All caught up in the heat of the chase, he was carelessly carrying his weapon by the end of the barrel. At the edge of the river bank, his rifle somehow got tangled in the exposed tree roots of the scrub oak. Cussing in frustration, he tugged angrily at the gun. The light was nearly gone and Gustafson was stumbling over things, trying to get into position to free it. What he had not realized was that an almost invisible root had threaded itself inside the trigger guard and, in a fishline-like manner, had neatly tied itself into a knot.

Gooz finally got a good grip and tore the rifle loose of the root. But he hadn't got his feet planted right and his backward momentum carried him past the oak and over the riverbank. Gustafson slid down it on his back, head first. Krieg Dabek pounced on Gooz as he went by, wrapping his huge hands around the man's throat and pulverizing his larynx. The pop-eyed Gustafson gaped back at his attacker, making strange gurgling noises. In a hurry to shut him up, Dabek crushed the posseman's skull with a rock.

Leaving the body at water's edge, Dabek crawled back up the bank. As silently as he could, he loosened a large dead branch embedded in dirt. It had fallen from the oak years ago and was partly rotten, but still solid enough for his purpose. Dabek started down the clay slope with the heavy branch, all of a sudden losing his footing on a greasy spot. He and the branch slid into the river with a splash.

Dabek could not judge how far the noise had carried. He lay stone-still in the mud at water's edge--listening. Several minutes went by. He finally heard faint human voices, but they were some distance away and did not sound alerted. Dabek got up and retrieved his turkey from the fox den. With Gustafson in one arm and the other around the thick part of the branch, he pushed off into the river. The current slowly carried them downstream.

It was dark now. At more than twenty yards, the makeshift convoy looked like natural river debris. Krieg Dabek floated past the other manhunters undetected.

7:00 P.M.
Constable Patterson's Office

Joe LaBounty closed the door and took off his hat. The room reeked of cigar smoke and strong drink.

"Well, well," Gordie Patterson said from behind his desk. "Look what the dog drug from out of the hen house."

"Gordie," Joe acknowledged evenly. He wasn't going to be

baited.

LaBounty looked around the office that was once his. The little wood stove in the corner was still there, a pitiful hunk of junk scarcely capable of cutting the chill on a cool June morning. The twelve-inch wide puncheon flooring was a little more worn but about as dirty as before. Gordie wasn't any better at housekeeping than Joe had been. There was a spittoon next to Gordy's desk. That was new; LaBounty would not have held with the use of tobacco in his office.

Joe noticed a folded pistol belt on the corner of Patterson's desk, next to the fountain pen stand. The leather looked stiff and dry. It probably had been lying around in a drawer for a good long while. LaBounty supposed Gordie decided to show it off while the Dabek hunt was on.

Joe looked closely at the revolver and saw it was a Schofield. Old Smith and Wesson model. Queer to see a gun like that being used anymore. LaBounty recollected Gordie's long fascination with Jesse James. Ol' Jess had carried a Schofield. Like a little kid, Gordie was. Had several books about their gang and once made a special trip down to Northfield to see where the James and Younger boys got shot up. Patterson, Joe remembered now, had got so carried away after his trip he went and bought the same gun for himself, though it had been no easy task to find one as so few were ever built.

Gordie must have hoped some of the outlaw's shooting magic would rub off on him. Truth was, neither Jesse or Gordie was a Latin Scholar. Practically nobody but hotheads like Jesse James ever carried the thing. While the Schofield was known for its quick reloading--the break-top feature allowed the ejection of all six cartridges at once--and used a .45 caliber bullet, the powder charge was pitifully weak. In Joe's opinion, it wasn't fit for stopping a grandmother at a quilting bee.

Gordie swung the castored swivel chair around and it broke out into the same old squeaky tunes Joe remembered. "I'm busy, LaBounty. What do you want?"

"I've hired on to protect Mrs. Prettyman. Thought I ought to report in."

Gordie sneered. "So you bought her tall tale, didja? Everybody knows she's got a bee in her bonnet."

"Dabek was there last night, you can be sure. He's going to try and kill her tonight."

Patterson slapped down the papers he'd been feigning interest in. "Got a real line on things, eh? What'd he call you on the 'phone and tell you his plans?" He made a dismissive gesture. "You're wasting my time."

Joe made no move to leave. Patterson got bellicose.

"If I was you I'd get out of town before the local law gets it in his head to work up a warrant for your arrest. Folks ain't forgot what happened, you ignorant Injun."

Joe shrugged. "Figured I ought to let you know there may be gunplay."

"Fine, fine," Gordie said, impatient to end the discussion. "You've reported in. Just one thing. It just came in that Dabek was spotted north of here an hour ago and they got him on the run. The last thing he's thinking about is old lady Prettyman."

Joe took a step toward the desk. "What do you mean 'spotted'?"

"Just what I said. Sheriff's deputies ran across his camp. He lit out just before they got there."

"Uh-huh. I take it nobody actually saw him." Joe could tell Gordie was hiding something. The Constable fidgeted with the paperwork on his desk.

LaBounty pressed it. "How many men dead?"

Gordie's head jerked up in surprise, as if to say how did you know there was trouble. "Gooz Gustafson is missing."

Joe tapped on his hat and walked to the door. "Gordie,

Gooz couldn't be more dead if he had gone over the Grand Canyon. What's more, Dabek is still loose and he's got business to attend to. He'll be along directly."

Patterson lost it, shouting, "What in the hell makes you so sure?" It wasn't clear whether he was asking about Gooz or Dabek.

Joe just shook his head. "Constable, your trouble is you never bother to acquaint yourself with the man you're hunting."

7:45 P.M.
Mrs. Prettyman's Home

Joe drank coffee while Mrs. Prettyman did what few dishes there were and put them in a cut-down wood fruit basket to dry. Mrs. Potter had packed a fine supper of fried chicken, gravy, mashed potatoes, and her own homemade white bread. Joe was full, but Annabelle determined to bring out a piece of berry pie. It was three or four days old and not much account, but Joe ate it anyway, to be polite. A few minutes later, Mrs. Prettyman excused herself to the little house. Joe watched over her from a window; he did not believe there was any chance Dabek would come this early but there was no point in poking Lady Luck in the eye.

There was a knock on the door and Father Aloysius Thornton strutted through. He had not troubled himself by waiting for someone to let him in.

"Well, well," he said, addressing Joe when he saw no one else was about. "It's true then, you're back." The Priest's smile was not sincere. "My condolences on the death of your mother. She was a good woman."

Joe said nothing. The bad blood between the two men went back a long way. Ten years earlier, when Thornton first came to Aitkin County, he paid a proselytizing visit on the Sandy Lake Ojibway. Joe happened to be at the village on one of his rare visits home; at the time he was a policeman in Cando,

North Dakota. Matters had not gone well. LaBounty was furious at this "man of the cloth" for suggesting the band's ancient ways were "heathen and savage" and ran him off in a most indelicate manner. As these things go, when Joe had his trouble in Balsam, what went around came around, and the priest got his revenge. The good Father became a leader in getting the townspeople worked up over Joe's "inhuman crimes."

"Pity to deny her a Christian burial," Thornton was droning on. "Even more her Bible and crucifix, so I heard," he said, his voice trailing away. Unexpectedly, the priest brightened. "But, no matter. I gave her last rites only hours before she passed and am quite certain she sits beside God in Heaven." The clergyman beamed so aggressively his gums showed.

Joe's bile rose; his temples throbbed. His hands were turning white from the grip he had on the back of a chair. If Mrs. Prettyman had not entered the room at that moment, LaBounty would have struck the man.

"Good evening, Father," she said, oblivious to what had transpired. "What is it I can do for you?"

The priest gathered himself up in a classic, superior pose. "Ah, tis the other way round, good lady. I have come to offer my services in this, your hour of need."

Mrs. Prettyman noticed the queer look on Joe's face. She addressed Father Thornton while looking at Joe, clearly wondering what had gone on between the two men.

"Thank you very much but, as you can see, Mr. LaBounty has taken me under his protection."

Thornton's manner grew stern. "See here, Mrs. Prettyman. There are a good many, myself included, who think it unwise indeed for you to make party with this man. Is it possible you cannot remember what he has done?"

She cleared her throat. "I am certainly aware of what he has been accused of."

The priest waved his hand dismissively. "Madam, I shall not be drawn into a debate over Mr. LaBounty's deficiencies. I have come to offer the comfort of the Lord, and to say that you would be much better off to withdraw your request for protection from this man and put your trust in our local authorities.

"Let not the devil enter your home!" the Priest suddenly bellowed. He poked his finger skyward. "Take heed of Proverbs 6 and 27! 'Can a man take fire to his bosom and his clothes not be burned?'"

Mrs. Prettyman's cheeks turned crimson, invoking the very image the pastor was alluding to. "Father, with all due respect, this man is my friend and protector. I will not have you sully him further. Good evening to you, sir!"

Father Thornton looked at the woman in confusion. He clearly had not expected this reaction. He gathered up his hat and, holding it close to his breast, made one last appeal. "Madam, I urge you to reconsider. Cast out this infidel and turn your cheek to evil!"

Mrs. Prettyman grasped Father Thornton's arm and firmly escorted him to the door. In an overly loud voice she said, "Mr. Thornton, if you wish to present your cheek to Krieg Dabek, that is your business. But I aim to do everything in my power to keep mine!"

8:15 P.M.
Behind Cayo's Livery

The padlock on Cayo's old shed was rusty from disuse and Dabek easily broke it open. He hurried inside, quietly closing the door behind him.

The town was dark except for a handful of low-burning lamps glowing here and there. From time to time, one would flicker when someone came between it and the window. Fortunately for Dabek, most people were tired from a hard day's labor and already in bed. It was unlikely anyone saw him enter town.

There wasn't much room in the cave-dark shed. By feeling around, Dabek located a large table and chairs. It became apparent someone had carelessly kept poultry in the shack. When Dabek ran his hand over the top of the table, it came away covered with old chicken-shit.

He wrestled one of the chairs loose and cleared a spot so he could sit down. He needed to rest as much as he could, save his strength. His entire body was quivering and his breathing was shallow-raspy. The frigid river had taken a lot out of him.

Dabek had dumped Gooz Gustafson's body into an old well and, after stuffing some essential items in his jacket, tossed the gunny sack in after him. He wanted to travel as light as possible from now on. Besides, all he was going to need tonight was the bale hook. He touched the point ever so carefully, and still it pricked his finger. He sucked the blood from the small wound, an act which produced an unexpected, and not unpleasant, warming effect.

He would not have chosen to come into town this early in the evening, but men and dogs were everywhere. There were many more than he expected. Somehow, they had found out his general whereabouts and he was in a general fog as to how that could have happened.

Dabek had always found reasoning some things out a real chore. He could not reconcile why it was easy for him to be able to plan his robberies and sporting outings so well, and yet get caught from time to time. He had several times spent time in jail for petty thievery. Once, he was even charged with murder--that had been planned perfect he was positive!--but lucky for him the law made some kind of a mistake and the judge had to let him go. He had never been in any real trouble until he was identified by Mrs. Prettyman as the rapist and killer of Krista Jorgenson. Now they were closer to him than they should be and he simply could not account for it. It didn't occur to Krieg Dabek that Mrs. Prettyman almost certainly would have told the authorities about an intruder the previous evening.

On top of his inherent problems, Dabek's physical condition was worsening, making it even harder for him to think straight. He tried closing his eyes to force his brain to work better, but it would not. After a time, with his head throbbing, Dabek finally thought to hell with it. He would trust his instincts.

He folded his arms on the chicken-fouled table and nested his head into them. It would be all right; they wouldn't find him. He would beat them, as he had always done. He dozed, thinking about the pleasant moment later in the evening when he would confront and kill Mrs. Prettyman.

8:30 P.M.
Mrs. Prettyman's Home

"Isn't it time we talked more about this 'sitting duck' business?"

Joe had to laugh. The old gal was a chameleon. Weak one moment, strong the next--sometimes naive to the point of aggravation on one hand, then sharp as a tack on the other. A real puzzle. Joe cocked his head to one side and considered her, as men generally do any woman. She was no chicken anymore, but wasn't cause to turn away either. She must have been a real looker when she was young, though Joe had an odd feeling that condition had caused her more grief than good.

The mantle on the parlor's large kerosene lantern was about to give out, causing the light to flicker. New shadows fell on Mrs. Prettyman's face, somehow revealing yet another side to her; one filled with--what? Mystery? Untold secrets? Joe uncrossed one leg and recrossed the other. This was getting powerful tricky; as good as Joe was at getting into other people's heads, Annabelle Prettyman about had him beat.

"For now, ma'am," he said, getting back to her question, "remember to act as if you are alone in the house. Try not to talk to me unless your mouth is hidden from view. If I move about at all, I will be sure not to give anyone a look from the outside."

She nodded passively, accepting the hide-and-seek instructions. From out of the blue, she said, "You know, Joe, they say people are not always what they seem."

"Ma'am?" Another zigzag. Joe was getting dizzy.

Mrs. Prettyman slid a creamy-white needlework shawl from her shoulders, folded it neatly, and set it on an end table. She made a show of daintily tugging at the sleeves of her shirtwaist, all the while holding a pink handkerchief in the palm of her hand. "Take yourself," she went on. "Everyone thinks you're a cad, perhaps worse. Some say you murdered that woman and baby. That would make you a merciless killer, no better than Dabek.

"But if that's so, why are you here? What is your motivation for helping me? And how does one explain your exemplary conduct before that alleged unfortunate occurrence? You know, the town surely has forgotten what you did for it. What is it about you, Joe LaBounty, that everyone is missing?"

She leaned back in her chair and smiled smugly. "You see what I mean."

Joe shifted uncomfortably in the overstuffed chair. He was facing a wall, an arrangement that kept him from view through the front parlor window. He had to turn ninety degrees to the right to look at her directly. At the moment, however, he wasn't sure how direct he cared to be.

Mrs. Prettyman had the wind in her sails. "Now take me, Joe. Do you think I am who I seem?"

Joe was truly confounded. What in the world was the woman driving at?

Mrs. Prettyman took a deep breath. "There is a very good

chance this will be my last night on earth. I think it's time I got a few things off my chest." She smiled without amusement. "To make my confession to the Lord, as Father Thornton would likely have it," she trilled.

Any time that man's name was mentioned, Joe LaBounty's blood pressure ratcheted up a few notches. "Mrs. Prettyman, I will not let Dabek hurt you. You have my promise. And there is no need for you to tell me things that are none of my business." The last thing Joe needed was to have the old woman spill her guts. That would only make tonight's work all the more difficult.

"Bless you, Joe LaBounty, and do call me Annabelle. We are comrades-in-arms now, are we not?" She took a long sip of tea. "You must not feel it necessary to treat me as a fragile old woman. I am not a stranger to hazards. I have faced them before."

There was another one of those other women again, Joe thought. This time there was a hint of steel, a suggestion of tempered world-weariness. He braced himself.

"Joe LaBounty, I was born Annie Klasterman, nine months after a Chicago chambermaid exchanged a bottle of rye for a night of sport. The last name was my mother's; she never told me, probably never knew, who my father was.

"When I was eleven, the Great Chicago Fire swept over the city and my mother was killed when a brick wall fell on us as we fled. She saved my life by pushing me away at the last second. I can remember nothing else until dawn, when another woman refugee threw a blanket over me as we rested on the grass in Lincoln Park." Her eyes fluttered. "I have been absolutely terrified of any kind of fire ever since.

"I lived in an orphanage until fifteen, when a couple took me in. They were among the most detestable people ever born to this earth. After a year of abuse--yes, you know the kind and it came from *both of them*--I could no longer stand it. One night, in great despair over what I had been reduced to, I took his shotgun and killed them both while they slept."

LaBounty's eyebrows shot up.

"I was caught, of course, and brought to trial as an adult. In the great miracle of my life, Mr. Nathan Prettyman took an interest in my case. He even hired a detective and lawyer on my behalf. I was dumbfounded, for by then I had decided I did not care to live in this awful old world any longer; I had even reconciled a date with the hangman. But Nathan and his men convinced the judge of extenuating circumstances and my youthfulness worked to advantage. I was in jail only four years.

"Mr. Prettyman visited often. Brought me books, taught me how to read and write. He hired a woman who showed me how to be a lady." She grinned. "Nathan was a man who planned ahead."

The words tumbled out. "You are wondering why he helped me? Two reasons: One, he really was a very nice man trying to prevent a miscarriage of justice, but two, and more importantly, he was insanely in love with me. You see Joe, Mr. Prettyman was a plain-looking man, completely unhandy when it came to the fairer sex. In those days, I was quite a beautiful woman, if I do say so myself. I am not ashamed to say I took every advantage of the situation. We married soon after I was released. He created a new identity for me and we moved out West.

"After many years, most of them good, we grew weary of the plains. It's such a bleak land and so far from anything. In 1910, when the Soo Line was put in here and Balsam was established, Nathan determined the town offered a unique banking opportunity--and he was right. He invested us and our nest egg in the town and we prospered, thank you very much. By the time we came to Balsam, I had come to the realization that I was actually in love with Mr. Prettyman. Our union became all the more joyous. I cannot tell you how grand our nearly thirty years together were, the only sad note being our inability to have children." There was a catch in her throat. "On account of the damage caused by my foster parents." Mrs. Prettyman dabbed at her eyes with the pink hanky but it was too late, her rouge was already running.

Joe had moved to the edge of the overstuffed chair, completely captivated by her story. He could only say, "Mr. Prettyman was a fine man."

Annabelle looked up abruptly. "I know he loaned money to your folks. The auditors had a duck-fit, but he just laughed it off." She paused. "That's why you're helping me, isn't it?"

LaBounty could only shrug, uncertain himself how to express all the many and conflicting emotions that had brought him to a chair in Mrs. Prettyman's living room. The only thing he was certain of was that absolutely nothing was being done about his own miserable state of affairs.

Annabelle ignored Joe's lack of response, having gotten completely wrapped up in her own story. "After Nathan's death, I was out of sorts. And very lonely. I didn't know what to do with myself.

"There were gentlemen, of course. One or two proposed marriage. I'm still not so unattractive, am I?" She fluttered her eyes.

"No ma'am," Joe allowed.

Mrs. Prettyman tilted her head coquettishly, milking the pathetic little charade for another few moments before continuing. "But I was frightened to death that if I developed a relationship with a man, somehow, some way, he would find out I was a jailbird and, if not a soiled dove, at least the next thing to it. And that would be the end of it; these Balsam gentlemen are hopelessly Victorian.

"It could not be kept a secret. At some unguarded moment I would blurt something out, or some piece of paper would arrive in the mail with incriminating information, or someone from the Chicago days would blunder through and identify me, or any of another hundred scenarios. And then I would certainly be undone, worse off than before."

Joe wondered if she hadn't overreacted, hadn't been subconsciously trying to avoid becoming an emotional casualty once again. Neither he or she would ever know.

"In self-defense, I created myself over yet one more time." Annabelle bowed her head regally. "Ladies and Gentlemen of Balsam, I give you the widow Prettyman--local eccentric, town gossip, and general busybody."

Joe was astonished. She had completely duped everyone.

Annabelle's eyes suddenly flashed. "Now, that son-of-a-bitch Dabek wants to take what little I have left, what few scraps of life remain to me."

With Joe still startled at the unexpected obscenity, Mrs. Nathan Dexter Prettyman stood to attention--back straight, hands clasped in front of her.

"As God is my witness," she said. "I will fight the bastard to the death."

9:10 P.M.
Mrs. Ostertag's "Blind-pig"

Rayno Randa opened the unlatched door to Ostertag's general store and followed the candles down the steps to the cellar. The eyeball on the other side of the peephole recognized him and opened the door to the illegal saloon.

Rayno tottered through the smoky haze to a table of familiar men working listlessly at a penny-ante stud poker game. Mrs. Ostertag wouldn't allow higher stakes for fear of trouble. She couldn't afford nuisances; her operation was already an open secret, only tolerated by Gordie Patterson due to the regular monthly appearance of a gold double eagle. Randa sat down heavily. This time, they would have to hand him the belt. He was a boiling mass of liquor-fueled rage.

The shame of it was--and when he was sober in bed at three o'clock in the morning, he could almost admit it to himself--it wasn't really Gunnar he was angry with. It was the man's pedigree. Torvald was a Swede, and if there was anything in the world Rayno Randa hated, it was Swedes and anything about them.

Randa's people had come from Finland, from a little Baltic coastal village on the western edge of the Aland Islands. It was but a stone's throw from Sweden itself, which was at the core of the problem. For hundreds of years, Finland had been dominated by either Russia or Sweden, the latter being the most recent. The Randas, probably more than most Finns and for reasons largely lost in the mists of time, had been nursing a grudge against Sweden for as long as anyone could remember.

Sweden's influence in Finland was so pervasive, Finnish children were required to learn the language in school. Rayno had a terrible time with the tongue. It just wouldn't come to him and he was mercilessly taunted by the other boys. It became one more thing to add to the long list of Randa grievances.

And now there was Torvald, representing everything that had plagued him in the old country. Never mind he and Gunnar had, he guessed, been "friends" at one time. All that went by the board when the Swede came between him and the girl. That had been like lighting a stick of dynamite.

Randa made a gimme gesture for the whiskey bottle on the card players' table and set her at full drain. A moment later his eyes bulged and he spat it all out. "Christallmighty!" Rayno flung the bottle to the floor, smashing it to pieces.

A nearby red-shirter guffawed. "You can drink Ostertag moon and get shot and killed but you won't die till you sober up." The others at the table chuckled.

Rayno raised a closed fist at the logger and slurred, "Shut your goddamn monkey-ass trap." He had already demolished a bottle of gin and was drunk as a fiddler. The logger shook his head slowly and quietly brought a glass of beer up to his lips.

In a sharp turn from where it looked like Rayno was taking matters, he suddenly bellowed, "Where's the asshole Torvald?"

Men from other tables glanced around uneasily. Mr. Ostertag, who had been cleaning up the broken whiskey bottle, moved cautiously toward a back counter where he kept his scattergun.

"I not so hard to find," came a voice from a dark corner.

Randa squinted through the smoky haze, trying to find his quarry. "Torvald, crawl out of that hole you're hiding in and show yourself."

"Rayno, you, I friends. No fight."

"Friends, hell. You're gonna wish you were never born."

Torvald strode into the flickering light of a kerosene lamp for all to see. Randa stood up to meet him. The Finn was well over six feet and well-built. In most circles, he would have been considered a very large individual, one that few would want to take on in single combat. In this instance, however, standing next to the incredible Swede, Rayno Randa had all the look of a St. Paul bookkeeper.

Gunnar Torvald had a full red beard, stood six and a half feet tall, and weighed nearly three hundred pounds. There wasn't an ounce of it working against him. It took very little imagination to picture him getting off a Viking ship and laying waste to England. "Rayno, I no fight you. This liquor talk."

"Bastard!" Rayno threw open his coat and drew a Remington .44 revolver from out of his belt. He had it at a forty-five degree angle to the floor, still coming up, when a chair crashed down and knocked him flat.

Smitty dropped the pieces of wood he was holding and picked up the pistol. "Rayno, I got a notion to push my fist in your face."

Randa struggled to all fours, his back throbbing where the

chair had struck. "This don't finish it," the Finn grunted.

"Gunnar, come here," Smitty said. The big man lumbered over. Smitty glared at the both of them. "Tomorrow just before sunset, you two are going to meet down at the depot stockyard. You're either going to fight this out with your bare knuckles or shake hands and forget it, one or t'other. One last thing. If there's any more of this kind of business," he said, waving the Remington over his head, "we'll hang the live one."

Rayno mumbled something that sounded like he understood.

Gunnar looked at Smitty and said, "Rayno always been friend. He forget when sober up."

Rayno staggered to his feet and scowled at the big Swede. "You just make sure you're at the stockyard at six." With that, he stomped out.

9:30 P.M.
Haakonson Farm

Charlie was still awake. His stomach was growling so loud one of his sisters pulled the curtain back from her corner of the loft bedroom and yelled at him. "Shut up yourself, stupid girl," Charlie said, with more hostility than he intended.

His Pa was down by the fireplace smoking his pipe. In a gruff voice, the old man shouted upstairs, "One more word, boy, and I take belt to backside!"

Charlie drew the blanket over his head and stuck his tongue out at his father. It wasn't his fault his stomach was so noisy. Anybody's would be if it was empty. As punishment for his school transgressions, Charlie Haakonson had been sent to bed without supper. He yanked the blanket off his head. It was so hot in the loft he couldn't breathe under it.

Charlie rested on his back in the little cot of a bed his Pa had built some years back. There was still the faint smell of the cedar saplings it had been made from, even after all the time gone by, and of the fresh spruce boughs his Ma stuffed each week on top of the slats and under the heavy woolen blanket he laid on. Now that he had gotten a lot bigger, his feet hung out over the edge. They felt funny, the way they kinda dangled out there. He supposed he would have to build himself a bigger bed, as it was certain his Pa didn't care one way or the other.

Charlie would have cried if he hadn't been working so hard lately at being grown-up. Why were they so mean? Why did they hate him? How was it that fate had dealt him such a bad hand? He always got the bum deals, had to do all the real work. All his dumb sisters had to do was housework. They had it easy compared to him. For the umpteenth time, Charlie Haakonson cursed God for not giving him brothers.

The only other worthwhile things the stupid girls did beside housework was the daily chore of taking care of the chamber pots, slop pails, and such. He crinkled his nose in disgust. Emptying chamber pots was about the awfullest job there was. Truth be told, he was plenty glad he didn't have to do that!

After a time, all but one lantern winked out in the room below. Anker tapped his pipe clean on an andiron, the sound seemingly louder than usual in the hushed house. In a much softer tone than he had used on Charlie earlier, he said, "Bedtime, Mamma."

Charlie was almost asleep when he heard someone coming up to the loft. His mother moved surely in the absolute dark, knowing exactly where every object in her home was. Ragna placed a wood bowl and spoon on Charlie's chest and, without a word, quickly beat it down the ladder.

Charlie sat up and shoveled the stuff into his mouth. Mush never tasted so good.

11:00 P.M.
Wakefield Hotel

When Kaymaki turned over, the bedspring squeaked like it was headquarters for an army of mice. The sound carried well down the hallway and she could have sworn she heard a snicker. Kaymaki groaned. What would the other lodgers think!

The mattress wasn't any great shakes either; it had several hard lumps and smelled of must. Mrs. Wakefield had neglected to air it out last spring and so of course Kaymaki had to pay the price.

It was high time she got a better bed. She had spoken to Mrs. Wakefield about it before, a number of times, but so far nay results. The longer Kaymaki lay there and thought about the matter, the more she got steamed. She had been staying at this hotel during the week for the past three school terms and deserved better. She resolved to *insist* upon a change in the morning.

This night, however, sleep wouldn't have come, with or without a new bed. For as soon as Kaymaki got her head clear of Mrs. Wakefield, Mr. LaBounty jumped in. She willed herself to stop thinking about him, but it was of no use. It was so haunting, so scary, what Mrs. Prettyman had said about learning the truth of the charges against Joe. What if everybody, including Kaymaki, had gotten the whole business wrong? What if Joe stood falsely accused? She rustled the covers, very uncomfortable with a back-of-the-mind notion that she had let his race get into the equation. But even if that were so, she pointed out to herself, if there had been any evidence pointing to his innocence, it surely would have turned up by now.

Or would it? What if everyone, including her, had blinders on? *Or had them put on*? Kaymaki's forehead broke out in a cold sweat from the doubt. She rolled over again, and became infuriated when the bedspring concert recommenced.

She threw the blankets off and got up. After pouring a glass of water from the nightstand pitcher, she sat in a chair overlooking the gloomy black street. No one was stirring except for in front of Ostertag's. A drunk was wandering around angrily talking to himself. It was that big section hand that Kaymaki had absolutely no use for. He was the kind of hard-drinking Finn that damaged reputations, hurt all things Suomi.

She folded her arms across her chest and glowered at Ostertag's store. Honestly, why didn't Gordie close that place up? She reflexively glanced in the direction of the Constable's office. Oh, for heaven's sake, couldn't she stop thinking about Joe even for a moment? Using both hands, she drank deeply from the glass.

A chill ran down her spine. Until just now, until this very moment, she had forgotten what Joe had said to her on the beach at Sandy Lake. It was almost a blood oath, spoken in a steely tone she had never heard before. "It is the one that first told the lie that I would like to find."

Her mind reeled. My God! What has happened? What have we done! She gnawed on her knuckles and sobbed deeply.

The weeping was cathartic. A few minutes later, a thoroughly worn-out Kaymaki was sound asleep in the chair.

1:30 A.M., Saturday, Columbus Day, October 12, 1918
Mrs. Prettyman's Home

Joe LaBounty finally relaxed when Mrs. Prettyman started snoring. It was very important to their plan that she fall asleep, that there be absolutely no doubt in Dabek's mind that it was genuine slumber and she wasn't faking. If he sensed her faking, and he was very good at that sort of thing, that would be the end of it. He would bolt the trap and all of this would have been for nothing.

LaBounty never would have believed Annabelle could summon the willpower to push the danger to the back of her mind and actually drift off. It helped that she was completely exhausted but, all the same, Joe didn't know if he had that kind of strength. He still could not get over the wonder of her story.

He was sitting on a straight-backed chair, wedged in a washstand nook ten feet from Annabelle's bed. Well before supper, while it was still light out and the bedroom was unlit, and with the probability of Dabek having the room under surveillance very low, Joe rigged a white muslin sheet across the opening to the nook. In a moment of inspiration, Mrs. Prettyman pinned on a couple of doilies embellished with colorful candlewicking. From outside the house, in low light, it would look for all the world like a wall with two decorative hangings on it.

Joe would have preferred a closet to hide in, but there wasn't one to be had. Even in the best homes, the tendency was to use armoires, clothes racks, chests of drawers, and other freestanding furniture. Due to custom, and in some cases because of property tax laws that considered all "rooms" liable for assessment, closets were relatively rare.

Joe had cut three small observation holes in the sheet, from which he could view any part of the bedroom. His holster was hung over the chair back, the Colt just inches from his right hand. There was a chamber pot and a pitcher of water within reaching distance. Joe had determined not to leave the chair for even a single moment before sunrise.

He had been in position since ten, Mrs. Prettyman's customary bedtime. The combination of the stuffy room and tension had produced a thin sheen of sweat on his face. He was already tired and not looking forward to an even longer wait. Joe expected Dabek between three and five A.M., but could not afford to be unprepared at any time during the night.

His plan was simplicity itself. The instant Dabek showed himself, Joe was going to drill him. No nonsense like "throw up your hands" or "I'm taking you in for trial." He would give this man absolutely no chance whatsoever.

Joe LaBounty was one of the few men who understood how *incredibly* dangerous Krieg Dabek was.

There was one thing unresolved. LaBounty wasn't sure which direction the killer would come from. There were two windows in the bedroom, on opposite sides of the bed. Joe left them unlocked, as they had been on Dabek's first visit. But they were unlikely entry points on account of Dabek would need a ladder and he would be in the open. Also, he might easily make enough racket to wake the woman.

Still, Dabek might try the window. As fiendishly clever as he sometimes was, he had blind spots and often did dumb things. All the same, Joe was betting on entry through the bedroom door, the only other way to Mrs. Prettyman, the way the man entered the first time. Joe purposely left it ajar, so Dabek wouldn't accidentally spook himself with a noisy entrance. Whichever way he came, Joe wanted him framed in either the window or door. As soon as Dabek was in full view, Joe would open fire.

LaBounty stood up from the chair in a half-crouch to get the circulation back in his legs. He rubbed his sore rear, cursing himself for not thinking of a cushion.

3:07 A.M.
Outside Mrs. Prettyman's Home

Dabek was not completely in control of himself. Despite a fitful series of catnaps during the evening, he still was very tired. And he couldn't stop shivering. That disturbed him because he had always been tough, always had been inured to hardship. He did not understand the icy waters of the Dead Moose River and the chilly night air had lowered his body temperature to a dangerous level. Krieg Dabek was suffering from hypothermia.

He continued to watch the Prettyman house, rocking back and forth on the balls of his feet and rubbing his hands together. It was awful hard to think. Last night he had gone through a cellar window, using the house stairs to reach her room. He saw no need to change that routine. Besides, that way he would not get lost in the house, maybe trip over something and kick up a ruckus. Yes, it was best to do it the same way.

Dabek began to blink rapidly and his head wobbled oddly. His body trembled violently for what he thought was but a few moments, but was nearer two minutes. When he came out of it he felt queer and disoriented, no longer able to remember how long he'd been staring at the house.

However long it was, he convinced himself, it had to have been sufficient to establish the fact that she was alone and asleep. No lights had come on since the lamp went out in her bedroom. There had been no movement inside and no sign of anyone coming in or going out of the building. Almost certainly the coast was clear, but Dabek would wait just a little longer. In order to make positive sure. Using the same caution he had with the posse at the river.

Once more, he tried to think of any threats other than the men hunting him out in the country. For the briefest moment, a wink of time, he wondered whether what he had done last night at Mrs. Prettyman's could have alerted the law. But the idea was instantly jolted from him when a dog started barking. The sound unnerved him. It was too risky to wait any longer. He must move now! He snatched up the bale hook and scuttled toward the basement window.

3:18 A.M.
Mrs. Prettyman's Bedroom

Joe LaBounty had been close to nodding off when the fourth step from the top of the stairs creaked. It wasn't much of a creak, more like a tiny squeak, inaudible to anyone not listening for it. Earlier, LaBounty had loosened the board in such a way so as to cause the effect. He hoped Dabek would shrug it off as a natural condition and not become suspicious.

Wide-eyed now, Joe drew his Colt from the holster, very silently moved the chair aside, and planted his feet just so. He did not cock the single-action revolver, for in the dead quiet house, with the animal-like hearing of a man like Krieg Dabek, he might as well strike up a brass band.

Joe strained to hear a footfall but there was nothing. Not surprising. Dabek would be on his best stalking behavior. LaBounty concentrated his full attention on the bedroom door. The pupils of his eyes had expanded to their maximum capacity and, despite the heavy darkness, he could plainly see it.

Joe glanced over at Mrs. Prettyman, who continued to snore blissfully, which was an absolute miracle. Both of her arms were outside of the covers, and they glistened ever so slightly. This was good; Dabek would be able to see for certain she was in bed and completely vulnerable. Joe mentally crossed his fingers she wouldn't wake up. Just a few more seconds and it would be over.

At last, almost imperceptibly, the door moved. Joe strained to see. The door continued to very slowly swing open. Dabek would be able to see her arms now. More moments passed. Still nothing! Joe's temples pounded; the palm of his gun hand was moist with sweat. He tugged at the linen to lower his peephole to get a better look. There! Down low!

In one fluid, lightning-like motion, Joe LaBounty threw the sheet open, whirled around to firing position while thumbing the hammer back, and leveled his weapon on the shadow he hoped was Dabek. By the time the gun boomed, the entire exercise had consumed less than a second.

On a bright day, the powder flash from the Colt would have been barely discernible, but to Joe's dark-accustomed eyes in the black room, it was like a searchlight. He involuntarily clamped them shut. In the same instant, there was a ghastly shriek, followed by something massive slamming against him. Joe LaBounty crashed into Mrs. Prettyman's armoire, the length of his left arm red-hot. Dabek hovered over him, ready to strike again. There was another inhuman war cry followed by the downward motion of the killer's right arm. LaBounty snap-rolled to his right a split-instant before a bale hook sank into the wardrobe only inches from his head.

Dabek tried to free the hook but he had sunk it so deep it wouldn't let loose. In a blind rage, he let fly a vicious backhand that sent LaBounty reeling against a wall. Screeching all the way down the steps, Dabek crashed through the front door and ran into the night.

Joe struggled to his knees, holding his blood-drenched, limp left arm. After gulping a few deep breaths, he tried to get to his feet. The room promptly went into a spin.

4:08 A.M.
Mrs. Prettyman's Bedroom

Annabelle held the water glass to Joe's lips. He took a few sips and laid his head back on her pillow.

"How long have I been out?" he croaked.

Mrs. Prettyman was too relieved to answer. "You took an awful beating." She ruffled air into the pillow so his head was up a little higher. "Gordie got here a few minutes ago and put you in bed. Are you up to talking to him?" Joe groaned, nodding once.

Annabelle called out and Patterson came into the room, stepping up to the bed. "Dabek?"

"Yeah. I don't see how I missed him."

Patterson pointed to a red-splotched rug by the door. "You didn't. Fresh blood there and down the steps."

Annabelle stepped into the light by the bed. "I heard the gun go off and this screaming that sounded like it came straight from Hades. I hope to God I never hear anything like that again."

Joe grimaced in pain when he propped himself up on his good elbow. The side of his face was numb from where Dabek hit him and he had a splitting headache.

"Feel like I'm gonna puke," Joe said. He swung his legs to the floor.

"Wouldn't try to stand up just yet," Gordie said. "I sent for help."

Joe waved a hand irritably. "What are you doing about Dabek? You won't get him jawing with me."

Gordie growled back. "Don't tell me how to do my job, LaBounty." The Constable belligerently adjusted his Schofield pistol belt. He had taken to wearing it openly since Gustafson had disappeared and Dabek escaped the posse. "We can't get started til first light anyways. Got no idea which way the fugitive went. That's why I'm here, to see if you know how bad hurt the bastard is or where he's headed."

"No, on both counts. And if you'd been doing your job, you might have backed me up tonight." Joe was so light-headed he had to lay back down on the bed.

Before Gordie could respond, Mrs. Prettyman spoke up, "I think that's quite enough, Gordie. Maybe you ought to be running along. He needs rest."

"All right, I'm leaving," Gordie grumbled. To Joe, he added, "Least you could've done is put him down. You ain't even handy with a gun anymore, you sorry ass."

"Really, Gordie," Annabelle said, her voice unusually high. "You are a poorly mannered man to use such language in front of a lady. I can't imagine how you were brought up."

Suddenly, tears were streaming down her face. With the worry over Joe lessened, the shock of what had happened was setting in. "Whatever happened to manners, to courtly men who respected and looked after women? Where is the decency? Where..." She turned her back to the men and sobbed deeply into her hankie.

At that moment, Mrs. Potter bustled into the room, her homemade doctor kit slung under an arm--Doc Finch was out in the country delivering a baby. Gordie caught the woman's eye and tossed his head at both Joe and Annabelle. "I don't know which one needs you more." He slammed the door on his way out.

Mrs. Potter set about cleaning and dressing Joe's wounds. Fortunately, his arm looked worse than it was. But it still took thirty stitches to sew up the damage Dabek's bale hook had caused.

"Thanks," Joe said weakly, when she finished. He finished off a pitcher of water.

"You better sleep for a day or two, Joe. You're not out of the woods yet. If the wound opens, infection could easy set in. And you lost considerable blood. Rest, that's the ticket."

LaBounty was very tired and not inclined to discuss the matter. Before drifting off, he mumbled to no one in particular, "Wake me in an hour."

5:00 A.M.
In A Dredge Ditch One Mile South Of Tamarack

The impact stunned Dabek. Both his hands were still clutching the steering wheel of the automobile he stole in Balsam. He had kept the headlamps turned off to avoid detection and, while going around a hairpin turn at a high rate of speed, the wheels caught in soft gravel. He was dragged off the road and had crashed into a deep channel.

It was in fact a dredge ditch, part of a large drainage system that had been dug a few years earlier to make the lowlands fit for farming. Now nearly empty of water--the swamps were bone-dry--the car fell a full ten feet before hitting the bottom nose down.

Dabek tasted salt in his mouth. He wiped a shirt sleeve across his forehead, and it came away soaked in blood from a gash he had taken in the fall. He ignored it, instead directing his full attention to the bullet wound in his side. It had gotten even more banged up in the accident and was aching something fierce. He was losing a lot of blood. Dabek angrily struck the side of the door. Where the hell had LaBounty come from!

He calmed down and took inventory of the situation. Except for that damn Indian, his luck had held reasonably well. He could still move, was still strong enough to keep going. He had not met another motorcar or wagon, nor seen any dogs or men, since leaving Balsam. The fool posse was all asleep when they should have been out hunting him. Well, that wasn't any surprise; they were only ordinary men, without the special qualities that he alone possessed. Their failure was to be expected and taken advantage of.

Dabek grabbed a blanket from the back of the car and ripped

it apart, tying the smaller piece around his middle as tight as he could. As special as he was, he had still been bad hurt. It was dawning on him that if he didn't get help soon, he would be in real trouble.

A light appeared above the rim of the ditch. Dabek peered up through the cracked glass windshield and saw a man holding a lantern.

"Hallo down there! Are you all right?"

Dabek decided not to answer.

"We're coming down!" yelled the voice.

A man slid down the bank and bounded up to the car door. A small lad was at his side.

"We seen you go over, mister," said the fellow, shaking his head at all the blood. "Our place is direct across the road. Going out to milk, the boy and I was."

Dabek moaned, and got the desired response.

"Let me give you a hand," the farmer said. He helped Dabek out of the vehicle and sat him down on the edge of the ditch. Dabek glanced to the side and saw the farmer's boy was holding a shotgun.

"Don't worry mister, we'll get you fixed up," the fellow was saying. He held the lantern up to Krieg Dabek's face for the first time.

The farmer gasped in recognition and lunged for his gun. He was too slow by half. Dabek tripped him as he started forward and snatched the weapon from out of the boy's hands.

The farmer and his son raised their arms without being told. Dabek moved over to the wide-eyed boy and put the gun barrel to his temple. To the farmer, he snarled, "Take me to your place. Try anything and I pull trigger."

6:05 A.M.
Mrs. Prettyman's Bedroom

Joe opened his eyes. The lantern was out but there was

enough light to make out objects in the room. *Light!* He sat bolt upright and, with head still throbbing, halloed as loud as he could.

Mrs. Potter hurried in.

"I told you to wake me in an hour." He tried to sound angry, but it came out a whine.

She looked relieved. "You needed sleep. And as my husband used to say when he was in a lumber camp, a body can't anyway get to work till it's daylight in the swamp."

Joe decided there was no point in carrying on a conversation about what didn't matter anymore and changed the subject. "How is Mrs. Prettyman?"

"Finally asleep in the settin' room. That woman's plumb tuckered out."

Without further preliminaries, Joe looked around, saying, "Where are my trousers and boots?" He was running short of time, prospects, and sociability.

Mrs. Potter wiped her hands on the white apron she invariably wore around her waist. "I don't have any expectation I can talk you out of whatever it is you're about to do, so I'll go get them."

Joe moved unsteadily over to the straight-backed chair where he had waited for Dabek. He got hold of his holster, retrieved the Colt from where it had been knocked into a corner, and sat down heavily on the edge of the bed. After catching his breath, he carefully inspected his weapon.

6:15 A.M.
Cloquet Union Depot

Conductor A.K. Easterday accompanied Mr. Rudolph Weyerhaeuser and his second-in-command Sherman Coy into Agent Fauley's office. The telegraph key on the latter's desk was chattering Morse incessantly, reflecting the increased activity up and down the line. Mr. Weyerhaeuser took charge.

"What's the situation, Fauley?"

"Well, sir. That fire over to McGregor has been up and down. Up again right now, so says the wire. There's another doozy up above us at Milepost 62 along the Great Northern line. That one is going to raise Cain. We got a fresh north breeze stirring."

"Can't we get more men to fight it?" asked Weyerhaeuser.

Fauley shook his head. "Every man left in the country is already out there. The well is dry." The agent blinked at his unintended double entendre.

Weyerhaeuser drew himself up to his full height. The son of the famous Frederick, Rudolph himself was no small noise in the timber business. A robust man, he was not in the least reluctant to get his own hands dirty, if that was what it took to get the job done.

"I'd like Art here to get together a Special first thing," he said. "I have no doubt there are a lot of men that need moving around to meet all these threats and that we can fill up the train. Coy and I need to scoot on over to our Little Falls operations. I want to make sure they are in shape over there and see for myself what's happening along the line. We'll look those fires over around McGregor and Tamarack and be back in no time." He puffed on his cigar, completely confident that his wishes would be met. "What is the road's assessment of the danger to Cloquet?"

The Weyerhaeuser family's Northern Lumber Co., and all its many subsidiaries, was based in Cloquet. Their mills and related were the major employer in the city. The amount of sawlogs and finished lumber in the Cloquet yards alone was staggering, totaling in the tens, perhaps hundreds, of millions of board feet. Worse from the standpoint of fire were countless piles of combustible lath, bark piles, and sawdust hills. The very thing Cloquet's life blood depended on--wood--was its gravest threat.

"Sir, from what I can glean from all the chaos," Fauley said, "it appears our city is vulnerable. I think we will be all right but, then again, if the wind shifts or kicks up worse . . ."

"Yes, yes," Weyerhaeuser said impatiently. "You can't make any guarantees."

Fauley pressed it. "The thing is, we can't afford to get caught out on this. George Stewart from over to Superior has ordered the Great Northern to start holding up trains here in town. He thinks by this afternoon he'll have four of them ready on the sidings. I'm trying to cobble together another from the N.P. There is an old locomotive loafing around that we think we can get steam up on."

Sherman Coy scratched his head. "I must not have got dealt a couple of cards. Why are we talking about all these trains?"

Conductor A.K. Easterday stepped forward. "Mr. Coy, if the fire does come this way, those trains will be the only way for eight thousand people to get out of the way in time."

7:30 A.M.
Haakonson Farm

"Charlie, you get to peeling fence posts. I start on oak."

Charlie picked up his hand axe and peeling iron and set to work. The cedar bark was dry and it was hard going. The posts should have been peeled when they were cut that spring, when the sap ran, but they had not the time to get to it.

The Haakonson's had nearly finished off a seven-acre stand of virgin oak. It was the last of the big trees on their quarter-section homestead, the pine having been long ago sold to the local sawmills. Five years they had been clearing their claim--Anker had only last month proved up--and nobody was happier to see the end than Charlie; if he never had to cut on a tree again, it would be too soon.

A gust of wind lifted Charlie's cap off his head. He raced after it but each time he reached out to pick it up, it blew away, like it had eyes and could make itself fly away just as he bent over to get hold of it. He finally stomped on the thing and pinned it down. The air was really kicking up for so early in the morning.

Charlie had no more than got back to his peeling when from atop the cedar post pile Jack T. Dog, who had appointed himself lookout, started a commotion. He was barking at a very smoky northwest skyline.

"Hey Pa?"

"I see it Charlie. Growing big again. Was almost out I tink. Wind come back."

Jack saw he was getting results and his yapping grew even more frenzied. Anker threw a big oak chip at him. "Pipe down!"

This was the second day in a row they had seen a big fire. Today's was more easterly, closer to Tamarack. Anker's face suddenly darkened, as if the shadow of a cloud had passed over it.

"What's the matter, Pa?"

"Vanderwater lumber. I forget about Vanderwater lumber." He was looking to the northwest, in the direction of Grayling.

Charlie shrugged. He had work to do. Axe in hand, he knelt by the seven-foot fence post and shaved a strip down its full length. Starting at one end, he maneuvered the curved peeling iron under the bark and tried to pry it up. After an immense effort, a brittle little chunk the size of a silver dollar finally popped off.

"God damn wood," he said under his breath.

8:10 A.M.
Downtown Balsam

It was a busy Saturday morning on Balsam's streets; the demand for wood products had reached a new high since late September, when at the Meuse-Argonne over one million

American doughboys hurled themselves against the German Empire. The piece-cutting camps couldn't afford to wait for winter to sled the stuff into town, so they were using wagons and even a few steam haulers, locomotive-type engines with two endless tracks similar to the new "tanks" they were using in the war. The haulers could pull up to ten or twelve heavily ladened sleds or wheeled vehicles. Most of what was coming in was cedar and tamarack cross-ties to be sold to the railroads, who seemed never to lose their appetite for sleepers.

There was a lot of other commerce as well. Drummers moved up and down the street from store to store, farmers were in town shopping, and buildings and homes were being erected all over the place. The ubiquitous tapping of the carpenter's hammer could be heard in every quarter of town. Down Main Street, the drayman's new Samson self-propelled truck lumbered along, bringing nearly everyone to the edge of the boardwalk to watch it pass. It was coming from the depot, its twelve-foot bed full of cast-iron cook stoves.

Kaymaki stepped out of the Wakefield Hotel just as the Samson passed by, and she marveled at it along with everyone else. There were almost as many horseless carriages in town now as teamed wagons, a fact which astonished her. Balsam didn't see its first auto until 1915; when the shipment got to town they couldn't unload them from the freight car because no one knew how to operate the machines! Now they were everywhere, taken for granted. After the truck passed, Kaymaki stepped down and crossed the street, dodging a number of boys high-sticking barrel hoops.

She rounded the corner by Ostertag's and stopped in her tracks. Joe LaBounty was standing in front of Cayo's livery, her objective, talking to Mr. Cyrus, the taxi driver. Unfortunately, Mr. Cayo was nowhere in sight. She stepped back against the brick wall of the Balsam State Bank, under the shadows of its deep awning, uncertain what to do next.

Last night, she had convinced herself she ought to have a good long talk with Mr. Joe LaBounty. Get everything out in the open. Find out what was going on! But now in the bright morning light, after a night's sleep and freshly torn between the new evidence and the old doubts, she wasn't sure a face-to-face meeting was a good idea, at least not yet. Her first thoughts when rising this morning were her talk with Gordie right after Joe had fled and how convincing his story had been. But at breakfast, she heard about Dabek's attack on Mrs. Prettyman and that Joe had defended the old woman. Had in fact saved her life. Kaymaki didn't know what to think or do now. She needed time to make sense out of what was happening.

But she also needed to make for the livery, for she had counted on the school trip to Tamarack to buy her that time. Unfortunately, the object of her dilemma stood in the way, jawing away with Mr. Cyrus in front of the livery door, with no indication when he might leave. She was stuck, and growing more uneasy by the second about loitering on a public platform.

At that moment, Mr. Cayo strode out of the bank under a full head of steam and nearly ran her down. Kaymaki instinctively trotted out her brightest smile. "Morning, Mr. Cayo."

Percy Cayo was his usual chipper self and gave no indication he had taken note of her agitated behavior. He took off his cap and swept it grandly from left to right, as if she were royalty. "Well, good morning, Kaymaki! Your machine is ready. Oiled and watered, gasoline tank full. I put in two extra tires in case of puncture." He slapped his cap back on and guffawed loudly. Once, during a bad rash of flat tires, Kaymaki had said that Mr. Cayo must be spreading tacks out at night so that his garage might have more business during the day. He always made it a point to keep the joke alive.

Percy offered his arm to Kaymaki and they strolled over to where stood LaBounty and Mr. Cyrus. When Joe saw them coming, he took off his big hat and began to spin it rapidly. When that didn't satisfy him, he took to nervously fingering the two top creases on the crown. The general look of his type of cover had come years ago as a result of the northern plains winters, when the old mitten-handed cowboys had taken off their hats by pinching the tops.

The four of them murmured morning pleasantries to one another, then walked inside the livery. At length, Joe directed a remark at Kaymaki. "That smoke up north looks bad. Don't know if you had ought to be heading up that way."

Kaymaki lifted her skirt and made for her car. "I have business in Tamarack."

"Can't it wait?" Joe asked.

Yes it can, Kaymaki thought. "No, it can't," she said crossly. "I'm fully capable of making my own decisions, thank you Mr. LaBounty."

Mr. Cayo looked perplexed. "Why Kaymaki, I expect Joe was only looking out for you. No call, really, to jump on him." Percy had a way of talking to folks that didn't generally offend, even if what he had to say wasn't to their liking. Then too, word had gotten round what LaBounty had done for Mrs. Prettyman and Percy looked to believe it had bought Joe a little consideration.

Kaymaki flushed, putting her hand on the car door handle. Damn, she thought. This wasn't the way she wanted it to go.

"Yes, I suppose you're right." She couldn't quite bring herself to apologize to Joe. "But nevertheless, my mind is made up. Will you wind it for me, Mr. Cayo?"

"Yes'um."

Before Percy could make a move, Joe tapped his shoulder. "I'll do it," he said.

Kaymaki's eyes followed Joe to the front of her 1912 Reo The Fifth. Reo, for Ransom E. Olds, the maker. She had bought it with her own earned money and was one of the very few women in the north country that held title to an automobile. It would cost new some $1,000, however she had been alerted to a very good deal from a distressed seller and got it last year for only $250. Well, maybe "only" was too strong a word. That was nearly six months' pay and it had taken her a long time to save it up. But it had been worth every penny.

Hers was a four-passenger body, with a thirty horsepower motor. It had the more desirable left side drive, the way most new cars were going. However, it had not an electric self-starter and that was the hardest part for Kaymaki, though she was usually strong and patient enough to get it going by herself if there was no other way. But the rest was fine; mohair top, rugged side curtains she made herself, windshield, and even a speedometer. Aided by the careful application of Mr. Cayo's mechanical tools, her Reo could achieve a best speed topping forty-five miles per hour, which made it the fastest car in town. Most importantly, the automobile offered Kaymaki freedom to move about as she pleased, where she pleased, when she pleased. Just like a man.

She set the spark to the magneto and positioned the gas lever, making sure the vehicle was out of gear. Joe inserted the crank handle at the front of the machine and pulled it through with authority. The engine caught on the second try. With both feet on clutch and brakes, Kaymaki adjusted the wheel column hand throttle to a throaty idle and engaged the floor gear shift into Low. She held the clutch in while LaBounty walked around to her side of the car, dropped the crank in the back seat, and stooped down to her eye level. She looked at him, the thinnest of smiles on her face.

"I heard about last night," Kaymaki said over the puttering engine. "How's your arm?"

He rubbed it gingerly. "Feels peculiar. Hope it don't bust open on me."

"Uh-huh," she said, studying the bruises on his face.

"Appears you can be glad of a hard head as well."

Joe smiled that old 'ah shucks' smile and Kaymaki's heart skipped a beat. He could still do it to her.

"Yeah," Joe said. "Ol' Krieg is a mighty rough customer."

Kaymaki looked over at a well-traveled, black Model T in the corner of the livery. "Let me guess. You've hired Archie Cyrus and his Tin Lizzie and are going after Dabek."

Joe allowed a rare full-size grin. "Arch says that Ford of his will go anywhere except in Society." Then more seriously. "I tracked Dabek a ways out of town. Was easier than I expected. In his hurry, he must not have realized he was leaking a trail and failed to take steps to cover it up. Family out there said their car got stole early this morning. They think whoever did it headed up the Lawler road."

"Does Gordie know?" It would be just like Joe LaBounty to go it alone. She could sense the anger, the humiliation of letting his man get away.

"I stopped by the good Constable's office, but as usual, he has gone off on another of his bright ideas, where I know not. I can't wait on him."

Kaymaki's fingers danced on the steering wheel. She had to make some kind of a move here, and not just on account her feet were getting tired holding the car still. "Joe, it appears we are headed in the same general direction. Why not ride along with me?"

There she went again with that old forwardness, getting herself into more trouble. Kaymaki could have kicked herself for running at the mouth. She was even more surprised when finding out she wasn't finished. "I mean there is no sense in the world not helping one another when it's plain we can do so without a hardship to either of us. That is, in case there is some little trouble with the car or this fire business. Or some other difficulty that could rise up . . ." She stifled a little laugh at her foolish babbling.

Percy Cayo jumped in. "Now that's a capital idea. No telling what you'll run into along the way. I'd feel a whole lot better if you two stuck together." He fell silent when he realized what he'd said.

"Might be slow going," Joe said. "I'll be having to look for sign, talk to folks, try to figure what Dabek's up to."

Kaymaki pointed to the passenger seat. "Let's get at it," she said. Joe raced to the other side of the auto and jumped in, narrowly missing getting his foot run over when Kaymaki popped the clutch and the car sailed out of the livery.

8:15 A.M.
In A Log House One Mile South Of Tamarack

The boy took a step toward the door, grazing an arm on the heavy coats hanging from nails driven into the rough pine slabs. Krieg Dabek opened his eyes and waved the shotgun. "I said no moving." It came out a raspy growl. "You think to trick Dabek?"

"No sir, I need to-to-to," came the high-pitched stammer. The lad looked at his mother.

"He has to use the privy," she said.

Dabek shook his head. "Slop pail." He leaned on an elbow, carefully watching the boy go in the tall bucket under the dry sink. The lad stepped back and buttoned up his fly, and Dabek slumped back on the farmer's bed. The shotgun rested beside him, a single ham hand wrapped around the checkered grip.

Dabek grunted, flicking a bedbug from off his stomach. He was still groggy, but the hour or so of sleep had done wonders. Still, it wasn't enough. He tried to get comfortable but it was of little use. The bed had no springs; wood slats wedged into a rough frame held matters off the floor. The "mattress" was made of linen flour sacks stuffed with straw. For want of being nailed down, they proceeded to squirt this way and that without notice; even by Dabek's low standards, it was unpleasant.

The fugitive looked around the rude one-room hut. It was the first time he'd really taken it in. Most everyone else in the country had done well enough to get themselves up a proper house, but this fellow must have a pitiful farm, or was a pitiful farmer, or both. Either way, Dabek concluded, they were poor as church mice. He flicked away yet another grayback.

The owner of the place was but a few feet away, roped to one of the cookstove's clawed feet. The man sat cross-legged on the floor, head on his chest, whimpering. The goodwife was on his right, glowering at the intruder. She sat on a chair with her hands tied behind her and the chairback. Only the boy had been left unconfined, in order that he might run errands, tote water, and so forth. Dabek counted on his own uncommon hearing to detect any mischief.

With his left hand--the right being permanently welded to the shotgun stock--Dabek pulled back his blood-spattered shirt and inspected the gunshot wound. Fortunately, the bullet went straight through him. The wife had sewed him up pretty good; the bandages were tight and clean and there was no sign of blood seeping through. It was clear she was handy at doctoring, despite the fact her hands had shook all the while.

No wonder on that score, what with a shotgun between her legs from the operation's start to finish. There she was handling him all over, with her boy and man watching, and Dabek all the while having a shotgun jammed up under her dress aimed directly at the family credentials. Every now and then he would lay the cold steel against the inside of her thighs and she would jump. Of course, he had to be careful that didn't backlash on him, especially if she was throwing another stitch. But he couldn't help himself, it was too much fun; he'd lay the steel on her soft underside and she'd jerk. He wondered if he shouldn't have a little sport with her before he left. Dabek laughed out loud at the notion, and the three settlers looked back at him as if he had been kicked in the head by a mule.

The laughing had made him wince. Although some ribs were no doubt busted up, Dabek was pretty sure LaBounty's bullet had gone through his side without hitting anything serious. And the woman had been careful to use a lot of alcohol and hot water, so chances of holding off infection were good. The big problem remaining was the loss of blood. And the fact he would have to get more rest. First, however, he needed to take up the matter of the kid.

"Boy, bring cord and sit on floor next to Dabek."

The outlaw looped a length of rope around the youngster's neck, tied a choker knot, and drew it taut. The boy gurgled and threw his hands up to his throat, clawing madly. Dabek liked the sound of that and gave the line another yank. His reward was more anguished gagging. Krieg Dabek grinned. Holding on to the rope, he laid back and closed his eyes.

8:40 A.M.
Motoring To Lawler

"I'm ready to listen to your side of the story."

It came without any warning whatsoever, and Joe was staggered. Kaymaki had uttered the long-sought words; those precious, almost holy words he would have bet his life would never come. He felt disembodied, as if he were someone else, floating above two strangers and listening to their conversation. LaBounty rubbed his face vigorously with both hands. He had to stay completely within himself. There could be no mistakes; this was going to be his only chance.

"It was July the fifth, Nineteen and Seventeen. The day after the big celebration." Joe's voice quavered, and for a moment he thought it would break.

"I remember," Kaymaki said, in a manner urging him to get on with it.

Joe ran his fingers through his hair. "Your Pa come to see me. Never saw him so agitated. Shifted from one foot to the other all the time he was in my office. Said he knew all along I was no good. 'True to your own kind' is what he said, and that I ought never to call on you again. I was so taken back I forgot to talk. Expect he took that as confirmation of what he believed, and he up and left."

Kaymaki shifted the Reo from High down into Intermediate gear. Much of the corduroy, road foundation usually composed of tamarack logs laid side-by-side, was exposed on account of the township lacking the money for sufficient gravel. It was like driving over a washboard.

Her brow furrowed. "What time was my father in town?"

LaBounty had nary a clue what that had to do with the price of eggs but he was not about to not play along. "Early afternoon I'd say. After dinner."

"Gordie Patterson was out to our place in the forenoon looking for Pa," Kaymaki said. "I was home baking. I told him I wasn't sure where Pa was and he'd have to hunt him up himself. 'That's all right,' said he, 'I want to talk to him alone anyway.' I remember I didn't much care for the way he put that."

Joe shot her a glance and saw those old eyes flash.

"I don't know what went on," she said, "but Gordie left directly for Mille Lacs and Pa was in a foul mood when he came in from the barn."

Joe was beginning to see it. "Gordie was right in there. He riled your Pa up to set him against me." Joe cocked his head at her. "Patterson has always had an eye on you, Kaymaki."

Kaymaki said nothing, did not even acknowledge that she had heard Joe, keeping her gaze straight ahead on the road. She shifted the machine down to Low for a few moments, and then took it out of gear. In order to save on brakes, she let the car coast to a stop at the side of the road. The Reo had picked up the bad habit of overheating from time to time, even on short trips. They'd have to let it cool down a spell.

THE DEVIL'S HOLIDAY

Kaymaki was silent, had not even explained why they had stopped, though Joe had got that part figured out. She sat still, hands on the wheel. As if in wait.

Joe cleared his throat and plunged on. "I was mighty puzzled by your Pa's visit but got so busy with the drunks piled up from the Fourth of July that I could not look you up. I guess, too, I thought to let things settle down a bit. But that turned out to be a mistake."

He looked for a reaction, but there was none to be had. Kaymaki could be powerful mysterious in her own right. It was one of the primary reasons Joe had been attracted to her in the first place.

"The next day," Joe went on, "Sheriff Ike shows up and says that he had been delivered a complaint by a man from the Mille Lacs Indian village at Wigwam Bay. This fellow, he was an Indian, claimed that I took advantage of his sister and that a child had been born. He told Ike what with all the talk about me running for Sheriff he figured he owed it to folks to come forward on the matter. Well, you could have knocked me over with a feather!

"Ike said he couldn't believe it but went ahead and made an investigation anyway, only to find out, so said Ike, the man's story appeared to check out. The Sheriff went on to say he had been told of a letter from the woman herself pointing the blame at me. All that really surprised me, for I knew that such a letter could not have been written. Now I have always known Boekenoogen to be a first-rate lawman and I know he would never try to take advantage of that kind of a situation in regards to the Sheriff's race, but he ought to have got a letter like that in hand before charging off. Threw me off bad, as I could not make myself believe Ike had been taken in. I wound up giving a poor account of myself."

Kaymaki raised a hand. "You know, we kept hearing about that letter, but after awhile everybody forgot all about it. Come to think, I never heard of it ever turning up." She bit her lower lip.

Joe sensed the next few minutes would tell the tale between him and Kaymaki. "Well anyways, I'm standing there like a dope in front of Sheriff Ike and he goes on to say that wasn't the worst of it. This brother claimed, though he said he couldn't prove it and wasn't going to file an official complaint--that should have got Ike to scratching his head too--that I had contrived to get rid of the woman and baby by leaving them out in the cold winter night to die of exposure and then made it look like an accident." Joe had to stop for a few moments. He could not believe, even at this very late date, that a Warrior of the People would have to defend himself against such a preposterous charge.

"Ike expected the Balsam town council would ask for my badge just as soon as it could gather itself together. He didn't believe he could arrest me, for he had no warrant, at least not yet. He had decided to run on over first, look me up and hear what I had to say. Said he owed it to Tom."

Joe fingered his big hat. "Then the Sheriff really laid me low. Said he was glad Tom had not lived to see the shame his son had brought the good name of LaBounty." Joe had to quit from both want of wind and the bitter taste in his mouth.

"I remember you went to the mayor," Kaymaki said. "Said you wanted a meeting right then and there to clear things up. But everyone, including me--Joe I was in a state of shock! All of us were completely outraged. The evidence looked so conclusive, especially after Sheriff Ike gave every indication he thought you ought to be locked up."

She looked away, out the side window. "Everything was happening so fast." She quickly glanced back at him. "They said you had to run away from a lynch mob during the night." It was a question.

Joe nodded. "To say I ran would be putting it light. It

helped they got too drunk to be of any account."

He looked at Kaymaki. Her hand had gone up to an eye, had brushed away a tear, maybe several. He was sure of it. His heart skipped several beats and he felt lightheaded. *She believed him.*

With redemption in his grasp, Joe came to the realization the only reason he had come back was because of Kaymaki. He was very ashamed he had been ready to abandon his obligation to Mary, prepared not to come home, not to bear witness to her memory, not to be present at her funeral. Rather, he would have stayed and fought for what little he had left in Fargo. Fought for the little crumbs left to him, knowing full well that in the end he would lose those too. He would have done it, would have been willing to not come, would have been glad not to reopen the wounds, had it not been for one last chance to win back Kaymaki. On a certain level, he was ashamed. It was a fact that would leave him forever diminished.

But yet, a great thing had happened. Kaymaki believed him and it was going to be all right!

In this moment, this high water mark of his life, the sun blazed brighter, the sky shone bluer, and the reds and yellows of the maples and oaks were of a richer texture than any he had ever seen. Cranky crows had been transformed into songbirds and chirrupping squirrels bore the voices of angels. The air was so heavy and sweet-smelling he could believe a single breath might hold him for eternity.

Nearly choking with joy, Joe made a show of adjusting his coat and pistol belt, suddenly afraid he would wake up from a dream. Wake up to the terrible nightmare of before.

"We better be moving," he finally said.

Joe LaBounty reached for a large canvas water bag from the back seat. The radiator was cool enough so the cap could be opened. He filled it up and cranked the motor.

8:45 A.M.
Mrs. Prettyman's Home

Annabelle faced the looking glass and straightened her hat. It was a gaudy affair--black velvet with a multi-colored brooch ornament on one side and a long pheasant feather stuck out the other. It was too much, she had always known, but it fit her 'town character' image. This morning she determined to wear it because the old thing made her laugh a little and, after last night, she was in need of a little comedy.

Mrs. Prettyman stepped out on her porch and opened a purple parasol. She thrust it in the direction of the wind, in order to protect her hat and hair. The weather was kicking up again, unusually brisk for so early in the morning. A faint smell of smoke permeated the air, as it had off and on for the past several days. Though the idea of fires so close made her quite uneasy, it had become routine, and she was almost getting used to it.

Mrs. Prettyman walked down the boardwalk, smiling and nodding at various passers-by, twirling her parasol--perhaps a little too gaily. Folks returned her greetings with various queer expressions, as if to say did we hear right about what happened last night and how could it be so if you are out on parade?

She passed Maijala's meat counter, the dry goods store just bought by some new folks from back east, and old Matti Kovanen's combination dentist/barber shop. She waved at Mr. Tweedy, who was in front of the Post Office loading the A.M. Westbound mail cart. A little ways farther, towards the end of "downtown," Annabelle arrived at one of the few brick buildings in town.

The sign over the door, hung perpendicular to the structure, said *PENDLETON J. GILLETTE, REAL ESTATE BROKER*. In a corner of Mr. Gillette's window was a much smaller placard that read "Notary Public." Mrs. Prettyman opened the office door and walked in.

8:50 A.M.
Haakonson Farm

"Pappa, you can not be serious!"

Anker spoke to his wife calmly. "Now Mamma we yust cannot let that lumber burn up. Never will we get a new barn without it for there is no other money."

"But Pappa," Ragna went on, "you say yourself terrible fires up to Grayling. All kind of danger. Let wood go!"

Anker bristled. "No!"

He rarely raised his voice to his wife, but he was very upset. Charlie understood, surprising himself by realizing he didn't want his Pa to lose the lumber either.

As the moments passed, Anker became even more disturbed, both over his wood and the fact he had spoken harsh words to Ragna. He tried his best to soften things with an explanation. "Five years Charlie and I help Vanderwater cut so we can earn that pile of finished pine lumber. Too much sweat to let go." He tried to smile but it looked like he was in pain. "You see, don't you, Mamma?"

Without waiting for an answer, he turned to Charlie. "Get ready to harness team." Charlie was still digesting the stunning fact that for the first time ever his Pa had said "Charlie and I" did so and so.

Hooves clip-clopped from down the Haakonson lane, with the driver of the wagon halloing and waving an arm all the way in. Anker stood straddling his own wagon tongue, from where he had been hooking the harness tugs to the double tree.

"Johnson comes," he said.

Mrs. Haakonson wheeled and ran to the house, returning a few minutes later with the two girls in tow. Ragna almost threw her daughters into the wagon and then scrambled up the cast-iron steps herself. She sat the girls down on wood crates and busied herself with putting on their wraps.

Anker ducked out from under a horse. "What is it,

woman?"

Ragna shook her finger at her husband. "Anker Haakonson, you will not abandon us in face of Dabek, fires, God knows. We go as family or not at all." She set her jaw and stared straight ahead.

Anker looked to kick back, wanted badly to argue over the matter, but managed to hold off. Charlie knew why; when Ma got like this there wasn't any hope.

"All right Mamma, all right," Anker finally said. He wasn't even going to put up a token argument. "Maybe best we stay togedder anyway."

Anker and Charlie got into the spring seat. The boy picked up the lines--he'd been doing most of the driving for a couple of months now--and clicked the Percherons into a walk. The wagon turned and followed Johnson down the lane.

9:05 A.M.
The Log House One Mile South Of Tamarack

Dabek had slipped into a deep sleep and was in the midst of a convoluted dream. He was back in the courthouse, back to the moment when his lawyer told him he was going to jail for the rest of his life. Everything was the way it had been before except now the prosecutor was Mrs. Prettyman and the judge Joe LaBounty. Part of him sensed the need to awaken, to return to the real world. But he couldn't. The dream kept insisting he was already awake, that it was the dream that was real. The whole show was being fueled by the fever from his wounds; with the fracas going on in his head, Dabek did not hear the farmer's wife loosen her bonds and tiptoe to the telephone.

It was the crank, even noisier than most, that ended her brief good fortune. The woman tried to turn the handle quietly but the fact was it needed to be spun with authority in order to have any chance at all of a ring at Central. Unable to raise anyone, the unnerved woman finally wound it too hard. The operator's hello could be heard just as the earpiece was slapped from her hand.

Dabek let fly a vicious punch that picked the wife up off her feet. So furious at himself for allowing the woman to get this close to sounding the alarm, he took every bit of it out on her. There would no longer be any cat and mouse; he should have gotten rid of these people before. He picked up the double-barreled shotgun, forced it in her mouth, and blew the back of her head off.

The man and his boy watched in horror. Literally frothing at the mouth, Dabek emptied the second chamber into the farmer. When that did not kill him instantly, he clubbed the man to death with his own shotgun. The boy screamed insanely until Dabek, almost mercifully, bludgeoned him to pulp as well, completely destroying the gun.

Krieg Dabek stumbled backward, his head reeling. He was breathing in fits and starts, clutching his side in agony. The broken ribs stabbed at his insides like knives; he was pretty sure the woman's stitches had busted open. Dabek had to lean on the kitchen table or he might have fallen down.

His instincts screamed at him to get out of there. He remembered seeing a saddle horse in the farmer's barn and it gave him an idea. He could use the horse to get to Tamarack and sneak away on a freight. Dabek had always been able to count on trains; he knew the rails, the hobo jungles, the safe places to ride a car, how to avoid the bulls, how to keep from getting hurt or run over--whatever the railroad hazard, Dabek could deal with it. That's what he would do, then, he would hop a train. It didn't matter which way it was going either, as long as it was leaving these parts as soon as possible.

When his heart rate settled down to a tolerable level, Dabek headed for the barn. He passed an axe sunk in a stump, and on a whim--he was weaponless--gathered it up. He rode away without taking the time to saddle the horse. Behind him, the rough-lumber house door came under the influence of the stiffening northerly breeze. It swung squeakily back and forth, while dust and leaves blew into the lifeless cabin.

Krieg Dabek did not know he had slipped up. After he killed the family, he had noticed the telephone earpiece swinging on its cord, but he never connected the earpiece to the speaking tube. The line had been open to Central the entire time.

9:25 A.M.
At The Road Bend One Mile South Of Tamarack

"Is that the car?" asked Kaymaki as she peered down into the dredge ditch.

"Yeah." Joe eyed the Saxon stolen by Dabek. The rag top was still erected over the seating area, making it hard to see inside.

"Doesn't look like there's anyone down there," she said.

"Yeah." Joe reached his right hand inside his sheepskin coat and cross-drew the Colt. "Better make sure."

LaBounty skidded down the bank and carefully approached the machine. He saw right away Dabek was gone. There were many footprints, along with indications of a struggle. Three people--Dabek, another man, and probably a boy. Joe sized up what was written on the ground, looked over the car, and scrambled back up to the road.

He turned to the north and pointed at a farm a few hundred yards away. "He's gone there." Joe gazed at it for a long moment, then groaned.

Kaymaki asked, "What is it, are you ill?"

He looked at her with a pained expression. "I'm about to be." He added, "And so are you."

9:35 A.M.
The Log House One Mile South Of Tamarack

Kaymaki hung up the 'phone. "The operator heard the whole thing. Two gun shots, she thought. A lot of screaming, things crashing, more screaming." She glanced at the bloody carnage on the floor, then averted her eyes.

Joe finished his inspection of the bodies and covered them. "They sending anybody out from Tamarack?"

Kaymaki laughed mirthlessly. "Well now, won't you be surprised. Seems Constable Patterson was in town."

Joe's eyebrows arched.

"The telephone operator tracked him down right after it happened. He lit out for down here."

Joe was only half listening. "What the hell was Gordie doing in Tamarack?"

She shrugged. "Expect we'll find out soon enough. The operator said all this happened about a half hour ago so he ought to be here any minute..." Her voice trailed off.

It dawned on them both at the same time and they raced to the Reo. Gordie had an auto and but a mile to drive. He should have gotten to the farmer's cabin before they did.

9:43 A.M.
One-Half Mile South Of Tamarack

There was a bare-backed horse in the middle of the road. The reins dragged in the gravel as it walked nervously around a prone figure. The Reo came to a halt next to the animal.

Joe rolled Constable Patterson over and held up his head. Kaymaki asked, "Is he alive?"

"Barely. Get hold of your water bag."

Gordie licked weakly at the moisture on his lips. It was plain the man had very little time. There was a bloody double-bitted axe lying a few feet away. Dabek had sunk it into

Gordie's mid-section and ripped out most of his innards. What was left was slowly boiling out of the stomach cavity.

"Fooled me," Gordie said so feebly Joe had to strain to understand him. "Laid in road like a hurt man. I got out to help and he hit like lightning. I got off a couple of shots." Gordie gasped. His eyes fell on Kaymaki, who had knelt closely beside the two men to hear what Gordie was saying.

"Don't want to die without making peace." It was barely a whisper. "Mille Lacs woman was a put-up job. I paid them off, showed Ike a fake letter. Made sure it got lost later, would never had stood up in court. Just wanted to run off Joe, get his job..." His gasping turned to a raspy death rattle. "I wanted you Kaymaki... Stupid... Sorry, so sorry..." Constable Gordie Patterson let out a gurgle-sigh and then he was still, eyes wide open.

Kaymaki turned green and had to walk away from the grisly corpse. Joe called behind her, "You'll feel some better if you get rid of it."

Kaymaki didn't need persuading, retching her stomach empty in a series of great waves. She was doubly sick--sick at what had happened to Gordie, sick at what he had done to her and Joe. When finally nothing more came up, Kaymaki dry heaved, the strain so palpable she feared her heart would give out. Finally it stopped and her breathing returned to normal. Except for the bad taste in her mouth, Joe had been right; she felt better, though a little weak.

When she walked back to him, he was holding Gordie's Schofield and shaking his head. "Gordie was a chump. Two rounds fired and both finding their mark, but there is no killing power to this pea shooter." Joe hunched down and pointed at a very faint pink trail that ended where Dabek stepped into Gordie's flivver.

"Joe, I'm so sorry."

He looked at her, confused.

"What we did to you. What I did to you. Oh good Lord, Joe, can you forgive me?"

He came to her, held her lightly against his body.

Kaymaki was sobbing deeply. "How could you want me back? How could you look at me without feeling hatred?" She rubbed her tear-streaked face against his coat. "I wonder if I'm worthy of you, Mr. Joe LaBounty."

Joe cupped a hand around the back of her head and drew it into the small of his shoulder. He held her very tight. "I will judge that. The matter is finished and we will speak no more of it."

She forced herself to look up at him, to see what he really meant, what he really thought of her. Was he joshing, making fun? Did he want to hurt her back? That Joe LaBounty was capable of revenge, Kaymaki had no doubt. She had seen that side of him, knew him well enough to know he was incapable of turning the other cheek.

She needed to look into his eyes, into those shimmering black eyes, and find out the truth. Kaymaki believed you could tell whether people were good or bad, whether they liked you or not, by looking deeply into their eyes. She stared hard into Joe's... but came up empty; all she could see was the inscrutability, that famous LaBounty impenetrability that simultaneously maddened and thrilled her. She reburied her face in his chest. From now on, she promised herself, she would take this man at face value, would take him at his word, as she should have done all along.

By unspoken agreement, they unclinched. Still sniffling a little and not knowing what else to say, Kaymaki asked, "What will you do now?"

Joe stroked the farmer's horse to calm it. The mare was getting thoroughly agitated from the smell of the corpse. "Gordie must have figured the fugitive might head this way. I had forgot Dabek mostly grew up around Tamarack, knows this country well. Probably has any number of holes he can crawl into."

He paused. "But ol' Krieg has made some mistakes. Getting shot a couple more times will slow him up." He paused a few seconds, watching a turkey vulture wheeling overhead. "I expect we ought to say that Gordie at least did some decent police work. And he had grit." Joe looked at the corpse. "Shot Dabek twice after the bastard killed him." LaBounty eyed the Schofield in his hand, then disgustedly threw it into the swamp.

"The question is," Joe said, "where has he got to?"

In spite of the upset, Kaymaki had managed to keep her thinking cap on. "I'll bet he headed to Tamarack. Drove down that vacant west side alley where no one would take note, ditched the car, and hopped that eastbound freight that went through a few minutes ago."

Joe gave her an appreciative smile and a tip of his Montana hat. "You ought to be working for that Mr. Sherlock Holmes."

10:01 A.M.
Lunch Time On The Soo Line Track
Four Miles Southwest Of Grayling

Rayno Randa was so out of sorts he didn't know where to stick himself. He sat--collapsed actually--on a rail and twisted the top off a jar of mud. It oozed rather than poured into his tin cup.

Smitty had been trying all morning to lighten his friend up. "Ought not drink that stuff," he said, "but instead sell it to Ostertag for roof tar." Rayno was enjoying his bad mood too much to acknowledge the joke.

With eyes squinted nearly shut to keep out the sun, Randa drank deeply. Like many from Scandinavia, Rayno first took a cube of sugar into his mouth, then sucked the coffee through it. He chewed listlessly on a slice of bread, having not had the wherewithal that morning to make up a proper sandwich.

Randa's head was still pounding. He cursed himself for having stayed up most of the night making love to a bottle of red-eye. To say nothing of what had been done to the gin beforehand, which must have been considerable.

The confrontation with Gunnar was a blur. The Remington had been an awful mistake; he could not make himself believe what he might have done had Smitty not stopped him. In a rare moment of naked personal honesty, Rayno Randa could no longer comprehend his anger at Torvald. For it was true, they had been friends, had known each other for a long time. Before Randa took work with the railroad, he had gone up to the woods every winter. It was at a Prairie River logging camp that he first met the big Swede. They didn't get around to saying much to each other until one day in the middle of January.

Right after the swing dingle left from having delivered their hot noon dinner, the two men were paired up on a crosscut saw. They had just finished cutting a four foot thick white pine and were walking to the next tree, when from out of the corner of his eye, Rayno saw a tree toppling toward Torvald. Whatever warning that might have preceded the felling of that particular tree had been drowned out by the general din of ringing axes, men shouting, and pines crashing to earth. There was no time for jawing; Rayno leaped at a startled Gunnar and wrestled him to one side. The top of the widow-maker missed by inches, though a big branch banged them both up. When the Swede realized Rayno had saved his life, he smothered Rayno with gratitude for the rest of the season. It got to be too much, too uncomfortable to be that cozy with a *Swede* for chrissakes! Rayno found ways to avoid the man.

In the spring Rayno left the woods for good, and since that time had little to do with Gunnar Torvald. That is, until the current dustup. Rayno shook his head in disgust. What really capped the climax was that the girl was no longer interested in either one of them, having taken a fancy to some Minneapolis drummer.

Randa was attempting to recollect what it was that was supposed to happen at six tonight when Smitty rushed up beside him. "By the living God," his partner said, pointing to the northwest. "Have a look at that."

A little annoyed, Rayno took his time turning around. What he saw made his skin crawl. There was a huge, mushrooming cloud along the N.P. track at Grayling, of a size and color he had never before seen. It was rapidly churning skyward, as if there had been an explosion.

The two section hands jumped on their hand car and made for Balsam as fast as they could pump.

10:03 A.M.
Vanderwater's Dugout At Grayling

"Whoa, team! Whoa!"

Charlie Haakonson couldn't hold them. He set the hand brake and jumped off the wagon, racing to the front of the team and grabbing both bridles. The big work horses were nickering and switching their tails nervously, alternately backing up and going forward. The wind was all-of-a-sudden blowing so hard, Charlie had to lean into the animals and spread his feet wide to keep from being knocked over. All kind of stuff was flying through the air; Charlie could see most of it glowed red. Ash particles started dropping like snow. Holding fast to the one called the Gray, Charlie peeked under his arm. His mouth dropped open when he saw a cloud of boiling smoke rolling into Vanderwater's camp at express train speed.

The Haakonsons had got their lumber loaded and were preparing to move out when it hit. Charlie's Ma and sisters were near the Vanderwater dugout, watching the missus pack them a dinner basket for the return to Balsam. The Vanderwaters lived in the half-earth lodge, half-root cellar structure when in camp. Anker and Johnson had been down by the sawmill, where they and Mr. Vanderwater were debating the seriousness of this new blaze. When she whooshed up, they hightailed it for the dugout.

Everybody was running every which way, yelling at the tops of their lungs. Charlie's team reared up and whinnied with even greater fear when they heard the alarm in the human voices. The din was so incredible Charlie barely heard his Pa cry out. "Mamma! Mamma! Get everyone to dugout. I go for Charlie!"

The Vanderwaters, Johnson, and Haakonson women scurried inside and closed the door behind them. Anker broke into a dead run towards Charlie, who was any longer only holding onto the bridles for fear the two nineteen-hundred pound beasts would trample him to death. Anker rushed to the team's side and, in response to a powerful instinct to save his indispensable horses, furiously tore away at the harness. He loosened the straps that fastened the hames to the collars, ripping the latter off both horse's shoulders. The belly bands quickly followed. The Percherons became more and more frenzied in proportion to Anker's fierce tearing at the rigging. He had nearly finished the job when a fire brand, this one a chunk of flaming two-by-four that may have been carried for a mile or more by the hurricane-like wind, struck Anker in the back and knocked him to the ground.

"Paaa!" Charlie's shriek was swallowed up by the earsplitting roar.

The horses had taken all they could and proceeded to lose their senses. Both reared in opposite directions; the one Charlie had hold of lifted him several feet off the ground. Despite the desperate thrashing and twisting, the horses could not free themselves, and they squealed uncontrollably.

Charlie was being brutally snapped up and down, feeling like the last boy on the world's biggest crack-the-whip line, when finally, providentially, he was flipped head over heels onto the back of the Gray. He had let go of the bridle just before his arm would have been broken. Laying astride the huge animal, he grabbed two fistfuls of mane and instinctively seated himself. Through smoke-teared eyes, he saw his father back in the rigging, tearing at the lines.

"Charlie, ride east," Anker was choking on smoke. "Ride east, get away, get-!"

The Gray had sensed it was nearly loose. With an incredibly powerful lunge, the animal blasted away the last of the traces and straps, and bolted free. In that last instant, the big gelding's left hoof kicked insanely at one final bit of leather wrapped around its leg, catching Anker square in the forehead. Charlie looked back and saw his father crumple to the dirt in what could only have been a mortal blow.

Charlie wanted to scream out in anguish, wanted to get off and help his Pa, wanted this terrible madness to stop. Please, please dear God let it stop! Make it all stop!! But he could do nothing, absolutely nothing, except hang on to the runaway.

Charlie hunkered down jockey style, fingers interlaced into the thick mane, his legs fiercely clamped around the back of the great brute. They were in a full speed, out-of-control gallop heading due east and away from the inferno. Though Charlie was not aware of it, only a short way back and himself at full throttle followed the always resourceful Jack The Dog.

Back at Grayling, in the hell Charlie and Jack were fleeing, the Vanderwaters, Johnson, and remaining Haakonsons huddled together in the dugout while the terrible fire raged above them. It was hot in the hut and hard to breath.

Anker Haakonson and the others believed that the dugout/root cellar would be a safe place to ride out the blaze, but they did not understand the dynamics of a great forest fire. An inferno of this magnitude continually demands greater and greater quantities of fuel. This enormous appetite for so much fresh air gives a big fire great power. Quickly and insidiously, the little oxygen remaining in the Vanderwater root cellar was sucked out and consumed by the conflagration. Not one of the party had a mark on them when they were later found; to a person they died of asphyxiation.

10:20 A.M.
Two Miles East Of Tamarack On The N.P. Track

LaBounty reined up the saddle mule he borrowed from the Tamarack livery. There. Something over on that clump of wild rose bushes. He stepped down to investigate.

Traces of gray wool cloth clung to the thorny plants; below them were drops of blood. After a few more steps up an embankment, on the opposite side of the ditch that drained the track bed, Joe stopped cold. In a moment of incredible carelessness, Dabek had left two huge pigeon-toed footprints in the soft, peaty soil. Joe contemplated all the signs, and then looked to the south.

Suddenly in a hurry, LaBounty clambered back up to the track bed and untied the reins from around a half-driven-in rail spike. He remounted the mule, goaded it into what passed for a gallop, and made for Tamarack.

10:25 A.M.
On The Shore Of Nelson Lake

Dabek rearranged a couple of crates and a wood snow fence in an effort to clear a spot in the duck blind. He had hoped to turn up something useful, but found nothing. One of the wood boxes wasn't quite so rotten as the other and he plunked himself down on it. He was thoroughly winded.

The blind was an O.K. place to rest for a few minutes--he had been running nonstop since leaving the track--but no more than that. He aimed to be on his way directly, put more space between himself and his trail. He had been in a proper stew, totally confused, when he jumped off the train. Why he did that, he knew not. It could only have been some instinct, some compulsion.

Over the last mile it came to him how much sign got left behind in all his hurry. His sloppiness was inexcusable and he shouldn't have let it happen. Now he had to trust to luck no one would run across his droppings. Becoming uneasy over the lapses, he banished further thought on the matter, in the manner he always did when exposed to his own weaknesses.

A ways back, he had passed through a sweet corn patch, taking time to shove a few ears into his pockets. He husked one and chewed absently, peeking over a wall of reeds at a farm a little way down the shoreline. This blind had likely been raised up by the owner.

As Dabek ate, as he felt his strength returning, he puzzled over why the wounds in his leg and shoulder didn't hurt worse than they did. The one in his thigh had got hold of a pretty good chunk of meat. For some reason, the slugs hadn't carried much kick. He shrugged it off. Getting shot three times and nearly freezing to death in the damn river, along with all the other general running around he'd been put to the last twenty-four hours, would have knocked out any ordinary man. But Krieg Dabek knew the answer to that. He wasn't any ordinary man; he was maybe tougher than anyone else who had ever been.

A chill ran down his spine. Dabek was suddenly getting a powerful new idea. A notion that would stand the whole country on its ear. They said he was dumb, but he was going to outfox them all. He was going to make it happen that people would talk about Krieg Dabek for years to come!

The notion was coming all in a rush. They'd figure him to rabbit. Turn tail and run. Just like those fools at the river. Hah! He would turn the tables on them. Even if they guessed he'd jumped a freight out of Tamarack, they would never expect him to get off right away. They'd be rummaging over to Wright and Cromwell and beyond, sending word up and down the line to keep an eye out. Watch out for Krieg Dabek, the word would go. Dabek's coming, run for your lives! And all the while he would still be in the country. Still going ahead with his original plan!

Dabek tightened the rag cloth wrapped around his thigh wound and examined his midsection, checking on the farmwife's bandages. There was a lot of dried blood, along with sweat stains and mud, but things looked about as good as could be expected. He buttoned up his shirt. Soon as he rested he would go on over to that farm place and look for some food and guns. Then he would head south for Balsam. Kill off the old woman once and for all!

He was struck by another pleasant thought. With Gordie out of the way, there wouldn't even be any law down there. It was going to be easy, a piece of pie!

Dabek felt giddy, and oddly warmed. His new prospects had even pushed aside the pain that had been racking his body. For the moment, his mind was as clear as it had ever been. After he finished his business with Mrs. Prettyman, he was going to immediately jump a southbound redball and leave these parts for good.

10:28 A.M.
Tamarack

Along with a number of other women, Kaymaki was eyeing the big fire to the west. Minutes earlier, a section hand on a speeder had come through and said Grayling was wiped out, and if the wind held steady Tamarack would be next. The fellow did not stay long at all, but had got right back on his velocipede and skeddadled to the east. Kaymaki and the others watched him disappear down the track, then looked back worriedly at the fire.

The women and children of the village were bustling about, preparing food and drink and trying to make themselves generally useful, while the men were gone to fight fire and plow firebreaks. There was no little amount of nervous energy; one woman made a pot of coffee, set it on the fire to boil, took it off the fire when it was ready, then proceeded to pour the entire contents on the ground.

Young boys and some older girls worked in relays pumping water into any manner of container and getting it ready to be carried out to the fireline. Several of the town wells were already pumped dry. The mail dray wagon had been loaded with gunny sacks, which when soaked in water could be used to slap out grass fires. A young lad was driving it out to the men. An injured, black-faced firefighter snorted as the boy passed by. "Trying to slap out a blaze like this," he said, "is about as satisfactory as shoveling straw into a stiff wind." Everyone's faces carried looks of quiet desperation.

Kaymaki wished Joe would hurry back. He hadn't said what he was up to, just made off down the track on Miller's mule, no matter her running behind yelling at him to say where he was gone off to. Aggravating man that way. She allowed herself an inner smile. Despite his contrariness, Kaymaki wouldn't want to be with anyone else in the world right now. In any number of ways.

"Lookee!" whooped a young woman.

A runaway exploded from out of the smoky gloom, coming from the west along the Black Diamond Trail. Several older boys ran out to try to bring the crazed animal to a halt, but it never gave a hint of slowing and they dived out of the way. The gray Percheron thundered down Main Street oblivious to everything except its own terror. When it passed the clutch of women Kaymaki was among, the rider fell off.

"Charlie!" exclaimed Kaymaki, as she rushed to him. A

couple of minutes later, a heavily panting dog loped up, nuzzling Kaymaki and licking Charlie's face. A woman pushed both Kaymaki and Jack aside.

"I'll doctor him," said Mrs. Mamie Nelson.

Kaymaki sensed the authority in the older woman's voice and did not argue. Only minutes earlier, another lady had told her that Mrs. Nelson, who appeared to be in charge of Tamarack with most of the men out fighting fire, had just wired Governor Burnquist to send the Home Guards. The implication was they expected to lose the town.

"Appears no bones are broke. Knocked silly though," Mrs. Nelson said. She looked at Kaymaki. "He kin to you?"

"One of my pupils." She was utterly perplexed. "I have not a clue what he's doing here." Kaymaki kneeled down next to Charlie, who was not coming around. She brushed the matted hair off his face.

"Well, I expect you will have to look after him," Mrs. Nelson said, standing up. "We have our hands full as you can see."

"Mamie, Mamie!" The Tamarack telephone operator rushed up. "I was making the calls to warn folks south of town about the fire and got hold of Dennis Carr."

Everyone waited for the rest, but Esther Steffer, stunned by the sight of an unconscious--dead?--Charlie Haakonson lying in the middle of Main Street, got stuck and couldn't say more. This was her second shock of the morning; she had been the operator the farmwife gave her life to reach. Mamie Nelson issued a baleful stare that finally woke Esther up.

"Dennis says there's a very dangerous looking man squatting in his duck blind on Nelson Lake. He had been watching him with binoculars when I called. Dennis wonders if it might be that fellow they're looking for."

Before Mrs. Nelson could respond to the young woman, Joe LaBounty clattered around the corner. He dismounted before the half-horse, half-ass stopped, giving it a slap on the rump. The mule sashayed toward Miller's livery; like all their kind, it did not need much encouragement to head for the barn.

Joe walked up to Kaymaki and said, "We gotta go right now."

"I can't leave Charlie." She cradled the boy's head possessively. She was a teensy bit irritated at Joe's abruptness.

LaBounty glanced around, sizing up the situation at once. Kaymaki could practically hear the gears grinding; Joe LaBounty was about as focused a man as there ever was when he was on a hunt. He pointed at the Reo. "We'll bring the boy along. You can tell me what's happened along the way."

He had been moving too fast for Kaymaki and she determined to catch up. "Where to? What about the fire? Aren't we safer here?"

Joe looked to the south. "Hasn't quite got to the Lawler road yet. Lotta smoke but we can get through if we move."

Kaymaki still hesitated. She was seriously confused. Why the Lawler road?

Joe picked Charlie up, his expression stony and unyielding. "We go. Now!"

10:40 A.M.
Driving South Out Of Tamarack

Kaymaki broke into the clear and exhaled hard, having been holding her breath. They had been in a bank of smoke only a couple of minutes but it had seemed an hour. A few more seconds and she would have gotten hysterical. She stole a glance at Joe, hoping he hadn't noticed how close a call it had been.

"I take it you've picked up Dabek's trail." Getting into the game helped steady her.

Joe grunted. "Doubling back to Balsam. We got to get there first."

Kaymaki suddenly remembered. "Joe, just as you rode up they heard from a man who said there was a dangerous looking stranger in his duck blind."

LaBounty head jerked up. "Who, where?"

"Ohhh, damn, damn. What did that girl say?" She scrunched her face up, thumping on the steering wheel as if that would jog her memory. "I can't recollect the name but I believe they said he lived on Nelson Lake. That's right, I remember because it was the same name as Mamie's..."

Joe interrupted her. "Turn left here. Nelson Lake is that way." Kaymaki complied as if it was an order from a general.

Lost in thought, they both fell silent as the Reo rumbled up and down the gentle, graveled hills toward Nelson Lake. In the back seat, Jack The Dog whined softly, accompanied by some rustling sounds. Charlie Haakonson was coming to. The boy struggled to a sitting position and spoke in a disembodied tone, "My folks are all gone."

Kaymaki and Joe were startled by the strange voice, having forgotten all about poor Charlie. Kaymaki was immediately ashamed of her thoughtlessness.

After taking a moment to digest what Charlie had said, she turned her head to the back seat, speaking softly. "Want to tell us about it, honey?"

Charlie stared straight ahead, unblinking. "I thought I hated them but I didn't. Now I ain't never going to see them again." He snuffled.

Kaymaki and Joe exchanged glances.

"I aimed to run away from them. Figured they didn't care about me. All the chores and such. But-but . . ." He rubbed his nose in a nervous reflex.

"But what Charlie?" Kaymaki asked tenderly.

Breaking off the stare, Charlie looked at her in torture. "Pa saved my life, made sure I got away, but then the horse killed him. I saw it smash his head in!" Tears rolled down his cheeks. "And when I looked back, the Vanderwater place was a furnace. I know everybody--my Ma, sisters, Pa--everybody is dead and now I'm all alone!"

Charlie looked beseechingly at Kaymaki. "I didn't really hate them, Miss Matalamaki. Don't let God punish me! I didn't mean it! I didn't mean it!"

The anguish was too much; Charlie Haakonson buried his face in his hands and bawled his eyes out.

10:50 A.M.
Dennis Carr Farm On Nelson Lake

The gray-haired man loped up to the passenger side of the Reo and stuck his head inside. The old batch had on a dirty union suit buttoned to his neck, the top half of which was covered by a faded blue flannel shirt. He hadn't felt the need this morning to put on any trousers. Kaymaki took the car out of gear and idled the throttle, feet on both brake pedals.

"Hello Dennis," LaBounty said. Joe had once helped Carr out of a fix when a couple of gypsies broke into his house and walked off with the old man's money box.

"So, it's true, you come back." Carr looked queerly at Kaymaki and scratched his days-old beard, trying to recall why these two didn't go together anymore.

"What's going on?" Joe asked, moving things along.

"That man must have a sixth sense. I had no more than got off the 'phone with Esther when he raised up from out of that blind, looked my way, and come a-runnin'. I skeddadled for the barn. He run through my cupboards, loaded up the Lizzie, and quicker'n you can say Jack Robinson was gone. I tell you what, I got a real bad feeling about that fellow."

"You did right steering clear," Joe said, in sublime understatement.

Dennis frowned. "Joe, he got the shotgun and my new Thirty-Ought-Six. Box each of Remington shells and

Springfield cartridges." Carr went on indignantly. "Rifle was a present from the daughter in Ohio. Had my name scrolled on it and everything. For deer hunting, you know. Dang buckshot don't carry near far enough. Now take that Thirty-Ought-Six, why she can take down a--"

"Dennis, I don't want to appear huffy, but we got to go." Joe nodded at Kaymaki and they sped away.

By nightfall, Dennis Carr would be shivering on a small makeshift raft in the middle of Nelson Lake, watching the complete destruction of his house, barn, outbuildings, and all of his livestock.

11:15 A.M.
McGregor Soo Line Depot

Northern Pacific Conductor A.K. Easterday pounded the Soo Line station master's desk in frustration. "Are all the telegraph lines down?" he asked.

"Yup," the agent said. "All 'cept to the west, no fire that direction."

"What about the telephone?"

"Same story."

The conductor lost his temper, kicking the closest wall. "You know we need the O.K. from your man in Duluth!"

"Ain't never going to come Art," the agent said calmly, looking sadder than a disappointed basset hound.

Easterday looked out the window at a Soo Line locomotive, parked on a cutout. Except for getting up a full head of steam, it was ready to go. The road had ordered it off the mainline, not knowing what else to do. Art, on his own initiative, had arranged the hook-up of as many empty boxcars as could be had around McGregor, along with a number of tie and cordwood cars used by the local loggers for shipping wood to Dakota. From the way Easterday saw it, these fires were going to drive people to the southeast, the direction the Soo Line train was pointed. He was convinced a lot of people were going to be trapped out there unless they got help.

Upon arriving at McGregor's other depot with his own N.P. Special, Easterday received word that the Northern Pacific had closed down everything to the east. His train would have to turn around and go back to Brainerd. Art left a trusted brakeman in charge of that short return haul, he being determined to stay in the game. A few of his passengers also decided to get off at McGregor until they could continue on.

Among them were Messrs. Weyerhaeuser and Coy. Only they hadn't gone into town to look for lodging like the others. The two lumbermen had attached themselves to the conductor and were presently in the waiting room, drinking coffee and generally engaged in some serious grumbling. Mr. Weyerhaeuser had made a point of informing Mr. Easterday he expected him to continue to do everything within his power to get them through to Cloquet. Or at least headed in an easterly direction.

It was while having a cup of coffee with the two magnates that Art shared his idea of a rescue train down the Soo Line. After noting that line's track was still clear all the way to Moose lake, Art pointed out he couldn't use his own train, for the intersection at McGregor had not been built to allow movement from one road to the other. It would need to be a Soo Line unit. As luck would have it, he said, there was one parked in McGregor, waiting to be taken up.

Easterday instantly regretted opening his big mouth to the two men, for after a very brief "argument" about the wisdom of their tagging along on such a train, it became abundantly clear that Conductor Easterday would not be telling Mr. Rudolph Weyerhaeuser what he could or couldn't do. Art did take the precaution of laying out the many dangers, but of course that had no effect. These were one-of-a-kind men, impervious to obstacles, manmade or natural.

The rescue idea had looked better to Art at first flush then it did now. The sobering question, the one that was foremost on his mind at the moment, was whether he should do the smart thing, which was nothing, or the right thing, which was damn dangerous, both to career and life and limb. Easterday artfully launched a brown glob into the spittoon and consulted his watch. With no way to get an official O.K., he was running out of options. There was only one thing left to do.

The Soo Line engine chuffed rhythmically as Conductor Easterday climbed the steel steps to the cab. It was an American Locomotive Works 4-6-2 Pacific-type steam locomotive, so-called because of the four wheels on its lead truck, six drivers, and two balancing wheels directly beneath the cab. Engineer Bucholtz was sitting on the left side bench, directly behind a small window that allowed him an unobstructed view directly down the track. He was dressed in "hickories," the traditional pin-stripped bib overalls of working railroad men. His cap was of the standard striped gray and white variety; his gloves thick leather. In front of him was the boiler back-head, along with a jungle of pipes, valves, gauges, levers, and signals. The fire box was at bottom center of the back-head, directly opposite the coal tender; the open box revealed a token fire. The fireman stood to one side, leaning on his shovel and staring at Easterday.

"Gust," Art said to Bucholtz, "I can't get through to your bosses. Looks like we're on our own. Smart money says take her back up to Remer but there are a whole lot of folks to the southeast that are looking at real big trouble. Far as we know, the way is still clear." Art paused, waiting for the engineer to pick up the ball.

Bucholtz bit off a chew of Spearhead and masticated slowly, looking out the window at nothing in particular. Well over a minute went by. It was clear he had it in mind to let Easterday do all the talking.

"It's risky to go on, that's true," Art said. "But it won't do nobody any good to turn tail and head back up north neither." He was still hoping for a positive reaction, but Gust Bucholtz was too old a bunny to bite.

Easterday sighed. He might as well get on with it. "I favor you and I, right now, taking this train to Moose Lake, picking up all along the way that want on. From the looks of things, we can expect quite a few customers."

Gust turned to him, finally speaking. "Your funeral."

Art shook his head in disgust. So be it, he was going to have to commandeer a rival road's train, and on his own responsibility at that. At least the engineer hadn't showed yellow and asked off.

"My funeral all right, and I may have a lot of company before the day is out," snapped the new Captain of the Train. "Bake a cake Mr. Bucholtz, and be damn quick about it!"

Easterday shot a look at the stoker. The startled, grimy-faced man grabbed his banjo and furiously shoveled in the diamonds.

11:20 A.M.
Heading Into Lawler

"My God!" The blood drained from Kaymaki's face. An orange-red wall of flame had exploded from out of nowhere and was swooping down on them with incredible speed, crackling and spitting with such animation she thought of it as some kind of rogue organism.

"Beat it for town!" Joe yelled.

Kaymaki jammed the throttle to the stop and gripped the wheel tightly. The vibration of the car wheels against the corduroy was so violent she couldn't keep the road in focus.

From the back seat, Charlie pounded Joe on the shoulder, yelling, "Behind us!"

Trailing the Reo by a quarter of a mile was a wagon load of

refugees making an identical dash. The four-horse team was pulling a freight wagon, with a whip-snapping driver, another man throwing pebbles at the animal's flanks, and ten or twelve people huddled in the box. The horses on the right side were stronger than the other two and the team was pulling unevenly, causing the wagon to lurch from side to side.

Kaymaki zipped up the little rise that led into the village of Lawler and stopped the car. They were temporarily safe, having crossed over where the men had ringed the town with freshly plowed ground. Joe, Kaymaki, and Charlie turned to watch the wagon.

The wagon's teamster stole a glance at the onrushing wall of flame to his right, and flogged the Belgians mercilessly. The blaze took on a renewed fury as if in response. Kaymaki blinked when the fire wave seemed to purposely swerve toward the wagon, as if it had seen its prey and was sprinting in for the kill. Several passengers clung to precarious holds and were very near bouncing out. A blanket of creamy-brown lather covered the beast's chests and their eyes had rolled a blood-shot white. Kaymaki eyed the time and distance between wagon and fire, and her mouth went cotton dry.

Only seconds from the plowed firebreak, when for an instant she thought they were going to make it, the wagon's front wheels collided with an especially thick corduroy log and the front axle snapped like a dry chicken bone. The wagon cartwheeled into the slough, dragging the horses with it. A heartbeat later, the fifteen-foot-high brush and grass fire swept over the wreckage. Human torches radiated from the pyre, lurching helter-skelter a few steps before collapsing into the grass ash. The high-pitched, tormented cries of the Belgians rang in Kaymaki's ears.

"It is too late for them," Joe said softly. Then very gently, he touched her arm. "We must keep moving."

Stunned past tears, Kaymaki complied.

As they made the lefthand turn toward Balsam, the car lurched heavily to one side. The right front tire had picked up a nail and was punctured.

11:20 A.M.
In An Oak Tree In Lawler

Dennis Carr's Model T had broken down when Krieg Dabek rolled into town and it took him a time to fix it. The corduroy roads were hard even on the tough old Lizzies; the radiator fan belt had come loose and he didn't have much for tools. Then he saw it was out of water and it took a while to fetch more. Fortunately, the people in town were fully occupied with the forest fire and nobody paid him any mind.

Despite being in an awful hurry to get going, he decided he had better see for himself about this fire. Figure out if it was any threat to him. Up to that point, it had been the last thing he had given any thought to. Dabek had only just got comfortable after climbing halfway up a tree to take a look when he saw a Reo racing toward town.

He studied it closely, sensing something. Somehow he intuited the car was pursuing him, understood it was after him. Like a thunderclap, and for reasons Dabek could not explain, he came to know the Reo carried Joe LaBounty. It was yet another of his many gifts.

How that damn Indian had managed to pick up his trail left Dabek bewildered, but he could see he had little time to dwell on the matter. For a few moments he had hoped the fast-moving grass fire might overtake the car, give him the break he deserved by destroying his enemy. But LaBounty and whoever might be with him had made it past the firebreak and were now watching a wagon load of fools trying the same thing. Dabek's finely-honed instincts grasped instantly the farmers didn't have a chinaman's chance. He grabbed a tree branch and pulled himself up a little higher for a better view of the fun.

What was he doing, Dabek abruptly thought, did he think he was at a picture show? He had been nearly hypnotized by all the action, fascinated with the notion of a ringside seat when a lot of people were about to get hurt. He had to get out of there right now; LaBounty and the Reo were nearly on him. He quickly slid down the trunk and made for Carr's machine, missing the wagon's fiery end.

Dabek held the steering wheel tightly, cursing the corduroyed road. All the jostling around was extremely painful; each bump jabbed a broken rib into his flesh. His thigh and shoulder were throbbing, and he was bleeding afresh from all three wounds. Despite the cool air, Krieg Dabek was sweating profusely; the euphoria he had felt when leaving the duck blind had completely dissipated.

Dabek forced himself to concentrate, to ignore his injuries and deal with the immediate threat. He must be very careful. Joe LaBounty was dangerous, the most formidable foe he had ever faced. He could never figure out why Balsam Town had gotten rid of him. Something stupid about a woman, he vaguely remembered. Women. He wished he didn't have to have girls for sport from time to time, for he hated them all with a profound passion. If not for his needs, he would have nothing to do with them. Sport and killing, that's all they were good for. Although he did not know it, deep within Krieg Dabek was a long-suppressed memory of being abandoned by a woman, left behind on a lonely doorstep at the age of six years, one foot chained and padlocked to the door handle of an institution.

Dabek became lightheaded and almost blacked out, forcing him to bring the car to a halt. He closed his eyes and rested his head on the steering wheel. The pace was too much. He had to force the issue, make the chase end. His body was screaming for relief.

The matter was clear. LaBounty had to be destroyed. Right

now. Dabek released the clutch pedal and the Lizzie catapulted forward, settling almost instantly into its herky-jerky top speed of forty mph. His eyes darted from one side of the road to the other, looking for the best spot for an ambush.

11:37 A.M.
East Side Of Lawler

Joe put the tire pump away and grabbed a rag to wipe his hands. The tire itself had been quickly changed, but as was often the case the spare had leaked air and had to be pumped up after it had already been seen on the car. And, as was often the case, the pump hadn't work right.

While rubbing out the grease, he studied Kaymaki, who was sitting on a large rock. The sun had momentarily peeked out from behind a mixed shield of high stratus clouds and low-hanging smoke, and she was basking in it. She had loosened the bun on top her head and her translucent yellow-white hair fell carelessly to her shoulders. From time to time, the stiff wind caught it and whipped it across her face. Each time, and in a patient, elegant manner, Kaymaki brushed it aside--not bothered by the little chore, the wind, the fire, or anything else for that matter. She simply sat there, gazing at... what?

Joe looked to see if she had spotted something, but there was only the high grass waving in the road ditch. Kaymaki pulled a long weed from out of the ground, a juicy timothy stem, and chewed on it absently.

Joe tossed the rag in the back seat and leaned a hip against the Reo. He guessed she was entitled to a few moments to collect herself after all they had been through. Kaymaki had proved up where not many women, or men for that matter, would have lasted. He remembered an old-timer once telling him about Finnish sisu, a kind of queer sounding word when a fellow considered what it meant. The man said it was something special the Finns carried within them that saw them through tough times. Something deeply embedded in the Finnish character--a blending of courage, stamina, perseverance, along with a certain stubbornness thrown in. No matter what the odds, no matter how bleak things looked, those that had this sisu never gave in.

Joe walked over to Kaymaki. Her face was smudged, the white shirtwaist dirty and torn, and the blue schoolteacher skirt thoroughly unrespectable. She had picked a small but colorful bouquet of wild red-stalked aster and goldenrod.

"Smell," she said, shoving the arrangement under his nose.

They had little scent, but Joe said, "Nice."

She smiled tolerantly at him and opened her hand. The wind caught the flowers and they fluttered away.

He told her they were ready to go. She picked herself up without a word and walked over to the Reo. He followed behind, watching her walk--posture erect, hands holding the long dress just high enough to prevent it from becoming further soiled.

Joe thought of their talk, of what Kaymaki had said about not being worthy of him. He had to admit that once the vindication came, after Gordie had admitted his guilt, ideas of retribution, of revenge, crept into his thoughts. He had thought of those who were quick "to cast the first stone," as the Christians liked to say. There were plenty to choose from, and the people that topped his list were ones like the priest Thornton, men who were always ready to tell others how to live while their own lives gave it the lie.

But Joe had decided he did not feel that way about Kaymaki. Not her, not any more, if he ever did. Hers was an honest mistake, an error born of great stress and disappointment, understandable when a person objectively considered all the circumstances.

There was also something else he had come to know,

something that mitigated everything that had come between the two of them. It was not her personal beauty, not their physical desire for one another, not even his almost painful longing to have her as his life mate, that had finally decided it, had at last allowed him to forgive her with all his heart. It was the fact they shared a spiritual, deep inner bond called *sisu*.

11:45 A.M.
West Of Balsam Near The Dead Moose River

The Reo's windshield exploded and Kaymaki screamed, letting go of the steering wheel. LaBounty and Charlie held on while the car ran off the road and hit a tree. They had been moving slowly due to chuckholes and exposed corduroy and did not hit with any more authority than to shake them up, though all three got cut up from flying glass shards.

Charlie cried out and almost simultaneously Joe heard the distant report of a second rifle shot. He had not heard the first one over the car engine noise. The boy clutched his leg, the blood trickling out between his fingers.

"Out of the car," Joe ordered. "Get down."

Kaymaki helped Joe slide Charlie out. LaBounty propped him up against a tire and Kaymaki tended to the leg wound. Jack Dog whimpered, rubbing his head against his master in concern.

Dabek had them at long range. Judging from the delay between the shot and Charlie's reaction, Joe figured he could be up to a thousand feet away. He had to be high up, in a tree. Joe poked his head up over the Reo's hood.

Spit... Crack!

Joe ducked reflexively. The slug had missed his face by only inches, putting a crease in the auto body and spraying him with tiny chips of dark green paint. Damn. Dabek was a better shot than Joe had figured; the trajectory drop alone on bullets from Carr's rifle, from that kind of range, had to be a good eight to ten inches.

While Joe tried to figure out what to do next there came a heavy rumbling, like long-distance thunder, welling up behind him. He looked back and saw a line of automobiles heading a dust tail that must have been a half-mile long. The reason for the parade was instantly apparent. To the northwest, rising hundreds of feet into the air, was a huge new smoke plume. Lawler was a pillar of fire and the townspeople were fleeing.

Dozens of machines were whizzing by the Reo. Joe saw his chance and scurried to the opposite side of the road. He ran alongside the automobiles, using them as a screen between him and Dabek. They were passing him at a brisk rate and Joe had to pump his legs as fast as he could to even have a semblance of keeping up. He hoped the supply of cars wouldn't give out before he could get close enough. Through the clouds of dust, Joe made out a big tree up ahead, taller than any of the others around it.

Puffing hard, LaBounty was just opposite the big elm when the last car zoomed by. Another shot rang out and he heard the slug whistle by. Joe belly-flopped into a grassy ditch and slithered into the brush. Just before he hit the ground, he caught a glimpse of Krieg Dabek on a deer stand about twenty-five feet up the tree. Joe had also seen, out of the corner of his eye, a dog flash by on the other side of the road.

11:49 A.M.
In The Elm Tree

Dabek slammed a closed fist against the tree trunk. He could not believe he had opened up at such long range. He hadn't been concentrating properly; his wounds, the general excitement of the ambush, and all the other distractions had conspired to make a complete mess of things.

He tried to recover, catching glimpses of LaBounty running alongside the cars, but he couldn't get off a clear shot. Dabek cycled the Springfield's bolt, chambering the third of the five available rounds. He brought the rifle up to the ready. LaBounty had to show when the last car passed.

There! Dabek snap-shot in the direction of the grassy ditch but knew immediately it didn't connect. He looked hard at where he had fired, then smashed his fist against the tree trunk again. That damn Indian had disappeared into the woods!

Krieg Dabek had liked the initial setup. He was pleased with the way the Reo was slowly coming in, the clear field of fire, the high ground, and, best of all, the accurate weapon in his hands. From the moment he first held Carr's gun, he knew it was an excellent rifle. A man like Dabek could tell things like that just from looking a firearm over--how it had been treated, if it was properly oiled, how the sights looked.

This particular long gun was a Model 1903 Rifle Caliber 30-06, built in the Springfield, Illinois Armory. It had a 24" barrel and an oil finished, walnut stock with a straight grip and grasping grooves along the sides. At a glance, it was not a particularly impressive looking weapon. Just another garden variety rifle to the uninitiated. But for soldiers or the serious shootist, the "03," so-called in recognition of the first year it was built, was the most reliable and accurate longarm in the world. Fighting men could have no better friend, as witnessed by the fact nearly 1.4 million of them were manufactured.

Dabek had matters well in hand, had in fact planned the perfect bushwhack. He had used a Y branch as a shooting rest to steady his aim, and it felt very comfortable. But for another fifteen or twenty seconds, just a little more patience, he would have had his quarry. The bad luck of the fire and cars coming from beyond and the intense anticipation of eliminating Joe LaBounty once and for all had caused Dabek's finger pressure to tighten on the trigger without him realizing it. He was astonished when the rifle went off.

Now *he* was the hunted. Dabek had to get out of the tree

immediately, for here he was a sitting duck. That was no easy target coming after him, no Mrs. Prettyman, no Gooz Gustafson, nor even a Gordie Patterson. That was Joe LaBounty. He carried a Colt and knew how to use it. Very dangerous, Dabek thought, unconsciously repeating himself.

He started hand over hand down the "ladder," a series of short boards deer hunters had nailed to the tree trunk. The pain, fatigue, and grogginess had returned with a vengeance now that his adrenaline rush was fading. He was bleeding profusely; the bandages wrapped around his side were completely red- soaked through. Moreover, the wounds from Constable Patterson's toy gun were finally beginning to take their toll.

While still ten feet above the ground, a weakened Krieg Dabek fumbled the rifle and it fell away. In his desperation to snatch it out of the air and still hold onto the shotgun, he neglected to keep his handhold. The fugitive hit the ground hard, noisily, and in great physical distress.

11:52 A.M.
Seventy-five Feet From The Elm Tree

Joe LaBounty heard the impact and the groaning that followed. He fixed the location and went after it, in the manner he always did when moving rapidly through the forest--not so fast that he couldn't control his footfall, never breaking or whipping branches, making no sound that was at all avoidable. He had a special stiff-legged gait for this kind of work, one that allowed him to almost glide over the ground.

Joe reached the tree quickly, but Dabek was gone. And while the Thirty-Ought-Six was there--the barrel had stuck in the ground like a mumblety-peg knife--Carr's 12-gauge shotgun was not. Joe took off after him through a gash in a hill.

11:55 A.M.
Dead Moose River

Dabek stumbled into the shallow river. With the extremely dry summer and lack of rain, it was only one or two feet deep. He splashed down the stream in open flight. Any rational thinking that he might have possessed up to this point had completely disappeared; he was now operating on gut instinct.

There was a tree leaning out over the river at an acute angle. Most of its roots were torn loose from the bank and it remained standing only by force of habit. The uprooting had created an opening in the earth. Like a threatened animal, Dabek jumped into the bolt hole. He smeared his face and hands with mud and leaves and, leaving very little of himself exposed, brought the shotgun to bear in the direction he knew his stalker would come. He sucked in great gulps of air, unable to catch his breath.

11:57 A.M.
Dead Moose River

LaBounty willed his body calm, directing every fiber in his being to hold fast, to not yield to the fear. He could be right on top of Dabek and not know it; the brute could make the earth swallow him up. Joe was in a crouch, at the edge of the river, very nearly motionless. He ever so carefully parted the narrow branches of a brush willow and peeked up and down stream.

Dabek's tracks ended at water's edge. Joe was certain the man was close by; LaBounty had stopped dead-quiet-still twice since leaving the elm tree. The first time he could hear Dabek crashing through the woods, and what could have been a boot hitting the stream. The second time, there was no noise, no movement at all. The man had gone to ground, determined to stand and fight.

Joe figured to work his way to a maple tree just over yonder along the river bank. It was about to topple into the water and the roots would give him good cover from where he could sneak up on Dabek, who had to be just beyond it somewhere. Holding his gun at the ready, Joe stood up and stepped into the river. It was a mistake of biblical proportions.

Carr's shotgun boomed, spraying Joe with #5 shot. It stung bad, but LaBounty was barely in range and no serious damage had been done. He silently thanked Dennis for giving up buckshot in favor of a real deer rifle; those were only duck loads Dabek had. Joe rolled up in the water to make a smaller target, putting his hands over his eyes to protect them from spraying B-Bs just as another round came.

When Dabek realized he was shooting birdshot, he became enraged. He roared out of his hole and attacked. Joe heard the deathly screech from behind his hand shield. Looking up, he saw Dabek was closing the fight, where his loads would be more effective. LaBounty steadied himself on one knee and brought the Colt around. He leveled it at the hulking, splashing figure bearing down on him and pulled the trigger. When the hammer fell, the black powder in the cartridge exploded and the .45 caliber round, a half-ounce mass of lead nearly one-half inch in diameter, burst from the barrel. The shock wave from the blast echoed up and down the little valley of the Dead Moose River.

Dabek staggered back, but did not fall, the bullet having lodged in the right side of his chest. He reflexively hip-shot an answering round at Joe, most of which caught LaBounty on the right arm and hand: Joe was swung violently around from the impact, losing his balance and falling into the river. Dabek started forward again, but this time he lacked the animation of his initial charge. His mouth hung open and the muzzle of his shotgun dragged in the water. He looked like some kind of mechanical creature, a great mass of unstoppable, unkillable, almost other-worldly being. He stopped ten paces from Joe and began bringing the shotgun up.

LaBounty had somehow managed to keep hold of the Colt. He was trying to get it up and clear, but his right arm wouldn't work right. Several well placed B-Bs had practically crippled it. The revolver was coming up out of the water, but it was taking too long. Dabek already had the shotgun stock nestled in his shoulder, nearly leveled at Joe's head. At such close range, even bird shot would finish LaBounty off. Joe could see he was going to lose the race. He thought fleetingly of his mother, of a tender moment when as a child he had hurt himself on his first hunt and she had kissed his little wound and sung songs to make the hurt go away. He saw her eyes, those ever kind and loving eyes...

A frenzied barking, a vicious howling, erupted behind Dabek. He instinctively whirled to meet the new threat, realizing at once his mistake. Jack The Dog, no dummy, bolted behind a tree.

In the time it took Dabek to swing the shotgun back around at Joe, LaBounty had steadied the revolver down with both hands. The Peacemaker belched flame a second time. Dabek was thrown back hard but, incredibly, still did not go down. Joe could not believe his eyes. There was no way for a man to remain standing after two direct hits from such a big bullet, shot from that range with that kind of muzzle velocity. Time stood still while the two men stared at one another. Dabek was holding the shotgun loosely in one hand, blinking. Joe recovered first. In the splinter of a moment, he cocked and fired his equalizer a third time, striking Krieg Dabek in the forehead. Like a just-cut great pine, and in what seemed to Joe to be slow motion, Dabek toppled over. Backwards he fell, arms high, as if he were doing a lazy backward flop off a swimming raft. Down he came, until finally hitting the water with a mighty splash.

Joe half-crawled, half-swam toward Dabek, training his gun

on the target the entire time. He wasn't taking any chances, none whatsoever. At five feet, the murderer twitched, probably involuntarily, and Joe unloaded the Colt into him. By the time the last rumble faded from along the river valley, Joe had rechambered, a painful and difficult process on account of his wounds. He nearly gave it up until realizing the reason the cylinder wouldn't spin was because, in the frenzy, he had forgotten to pull the hammer back to the half-cocked safety position.

Joe sloshed the final few feet and knelt next to Dabek, holding the revolver to the outlaw's head. His hands shook uncontrollably. Maybe a couple of minutes went by before he calmed down. Jack was splashing back and forth, snuffling and mewling, not convinced Dabek was finished, not believing it was over. But it was.

A still panting Joe LaBounty clumsily holstered the Colt and sat back on his haunches. The river water lapped at his hips. He looked at Jack and croaked, "Hardest goddamn thing to kill I ever seen."

12:07 P.M.
Soo Line Bridge Over The Dead Moose River

Art Easterday lost his balance and slammed against the caboose stove. Engineer Bucholtz had made an emergency stop and despite the air brakes on each car, the carriages still accordioned down the entire length of the train.

There was no fire in the stove, but the exhaust stack broke loose and soot covered the conductor. Art struggled to his feet and brushed himself off, attempting to regain both balance and dignity. The steam whistle shrieked and an uncharacteristically cursing Easterday bounded out of the crummy and raced for the locomotive.

He shouted up at the cab. "What in the Jim Hill?"

Art's voice did not carry due to the very high winds. He

yelled again and finally Bucholtz poked his head out and looked down, cupping a hand to one ear. The engineer said something back but Art couldn't understand him. Bucholtz pointed excitedly at the smoldering wood bridge not thirty yards ahead. Easterday could have kicked himself for being so slow to catch on to what was happening. He hustled over to the edge of the blackened trestle and made a quick visual inspection.

All around him, the wind was spewing flaming chunks of material into the atmosphere and spontaneous fires were breaking out all over the country. The firebrand that hit the railroad bridge had likely been a particularly hot one. Easterday glanced to the northwest, from whence his train had come, at the wall of flame only a few miles behind. The glowing evil was hot on their heels and growing larger by the minute.

He was suddenly struck by the fire's malignancy, as if it was capable of premeditation, of a specific, coordinated campaign of evil. His head told him that couldn't be so, that the thing was inanimate and would evenhandedly burn anything in its path. No matter something was good or bad, chaste or dissolute, hardworking or slothful, thistles or grain, it was all the same to a forest fire. It was a natural force, controlled by natural elements.

Yet, there was something about this particular malevolence, this ravenous monstrosity bearing down on them. Something ghastly. Art Easterday was a religious man, an unhypocritical Presbyterian; on a visceral level he could not begin to understand how a just God could allow something this hideous.

Something caught his eye. Art squinted through the chaos to the northeast, off to the side, along their flank. A fast-moving crown fire had suddenly exploded on the horizon--a type of blaze that burned across the tops of a dense stand of trees at an incredible rate, leaving the rest of the tree unscathed.

He scanned the unburned forest between the crown fire and the inside-the-Bessemer-furnace sky some miles back. Time was really running out now.

The locomotive panted patiently, clearing its throat from time to time with a pronounced *chuuuu-hahhh*, as if to remind Easterday there were pressing matters requiring his immediate attention. The conductor seemed to get the message and walked swiftly but carefully out onto the middle of the trestle. He looked it over, jumping up and down a few times, in the manner of a cautious buyer kicking the tires on an unfamiliar automobile. He earned himself a few creaks and tremors but, surprisingly, it looked worse than it actually was. While the fire had gotten hot enough to burn through the coal-tar creosote used as a wood preservative, it hadn't wrecked the bridge before the wind blew it out. All the same, Easterday's trained eye told him they couldn't take a chance; the fifty-foot span was going to have to be shored up before it could be crossed.

Easterday hustled back to the train to a clutch of men who had already been rescued along the way. While their families huddled fearfully inside the boxcars, they were milling about, waiting for a chance to do something.

"All right then, let's go," the conductor barked. "We got to truss her up!"

Art jabbed two likely fellows in the chest. "Hightail it back to the crummy and gather up axes, mauls, whatever you can get hold of." The men complied instantly. It was only after they disappeared on their errand that it came to him his 'volunteers' were none other than Mr. Weyerhaeuser and Mr. Coy.

Conductor Art Easterday pulled a large white handkerchief from out of his brass-buttoned coat and waved it over his head. He broke into a trot, running alongside the train like some Grand Army of the Republic general leading a charge. Over and over he thundered, "Come on boys, to the bridge, to the bridge!"

12:18 P.M.
Balsam

Kaymaki careened around a corner, dodging pedestrians, teams, and vehicles. After steadying up the wheel, she jammed the throttle lever to the stop and raced down Main Street. Unnerved at the contraption bearing down on them, a two-horse team panicked and ran away. The end gate on the wagon they were hitched to broke open and all manner of filled water kegs en route to the fireline spilled out the back and busted open. The teamster took after Kaymaki on foot, shaking his fist and issuing a long line of blue language, but she heard none of it in her rush. She rounded the corner at Front Street and braked the auto to a squealing halt in front of Doc Finch's office.

"Tend to the boy," Joe said woozily to the doctor. The physician had rushed out to find out what all the commotion was about.

Kaymaki nodded agreement. "Let's get Charlie first, Ted."

Theodore Finch was a recent University of Minnesota Medical School graduate. He had come to town with lofty, almost naive ideals, full of the need typical of his class to help poor rural folks. Surprisingly, and despite his sometimes effeminate, urban manner, he had come through for the town. Yet, after six months of long, hard days, infrequent pay, and poor living conditions--he slept in his office and boarded at Wakefield's--Kaymaki was sure he regretted not listening to his father and becoming a surgeon.

The doctor quickly extracted the bullet and dressed Charlie's leg. "You're lucky, boy. Kaymaki tells me the bullet went through her homemade heavy-leather side curtain before it struck. Between that and the range, it was largely spent when it hit."

Charlie looked up at the doctor, his face scrunched in pain. It was clear he was dubious about the extent of his good fortune.

To Kaymaki, Dr. Finch said, "My biggest concern is loss of blood. We have to get him fed, drink as much water as he can hold, and let him rest. Use the cot in the corner for now." With Kaymaki bracing him up, Charlie limped away from the examination table.

Doctor Finch addressed Joe. "Now, let's get you out of that coat and shirt and take a look at your arm."

LaBounty was unbuttoning his shirt with his good left hand when the outside door banged open. In trooped Mrs. Nathan Dexter Prettyman, heading a body of older men who had generally rusted out and looked glad to be led about. Before the door could be closed, a grizzled character by the name of Schmeissing breathlessly rushed in behind them. Schmeissing was a man who had been in the woods so long, he stared at folks with store-bought clothes. Kaymaki knew at once something powerful must have happened to bring him to this room. Several minutes later, the old hermit would proceed to tell everyone exactly what that was.

12:23 P.M.
Doc Finch's Office

Mrs. Prettyman had gotten her fill of all the confusion and chaos around her. Her old impulses had kicked in, survival instincts dearly earned and never forgotten. With the able-bodied men out fighting fire, there had been no one with any sense to take charge of the town so she made up her mind to take matters into her own hands. She gathered up the old men, all that were able to get around under their own power that is, and proceeded to get them organized.

The exercise, Mrs. Prettyman understood, was as much for its own sake, for the townspeople's own morale, as anything else. The fire was nearly upon them and the desperate reality of their situation was becoming suddenly and brutally clear. Without purposeful activity, people could get out of control.

Nobody had any idea how things were going along the firebreak, whether the men could stop the thing or not, whether indeed the loved ones at the front were even still alive.

There were foreboding signs. The last water wagon sent out had, only minutes before, returned driverless and with full barrels. The bale of gunny sacks it carried was undisturbed. Most ominously, scores of deer, raccoons, foxes, coyotes, and all manner of ground rodents were breaking out of the fiery gloom and bolting through town, oblivious to the humans.

It was these conditions, then, that had finally spurred Mrs. Prettyman into action. After forming her posse, she gathered everyone on a street corner and was about to begin a pep talk when Kaymaki's Reo sped by. Annabelle promptly marched the bunch of them to the doctor's office.

'Prettyman's army' was composed of old-fashioned men. While some of the people in town had gone soft on Joe LaBounty on account of what he had done for Annabelle, these old birds bucked considerably when they saw it was him. Kaymaki swiftly quieted them down. In a brief but passionate defense that betrayed her own guilt, she told them the real truth about Joe LaBounty. A couple of cracker-barrel philosophers, the real busybodies of the town--Mrs. Prettyman could not hold a candle to them, let themselves out the door to spread the news. All but Annabelle were incredulous over what Gordie had done.

"Not surprised, not for a moment," she said, making eye contact with nearly everyone in the room. "I thought all along that was the way the water ran. And now I'm here to tell you Joe is the man to get us out of this fix."

Joe rubbed his chin, mumbling, "If there is a way out."

The hermit Schmeissing raised a hand. In a thick, guttural accent, he spoke for nearly two minutes. A body could have heard a pin drop.

12:28 P.M.
Doc Finch's Office

Mrs. Prettyman smacked the doctor's examination table with her umbrella, startling even LaBounty. "All right then! There's a rescue train on the way and we're wasting time. Get cracking Joe!"

"He's hurt pretty bad," Kaymaki said. She pointed with more than a little concern at Joe's miserable-looking shotgunned right arm and bale-hook-slashed left. He looked like he had dipped them both in a bucket of red barn paint.

"Oh posh!" Annabelle said. "He's walking and talking, and by heaven that's all we need right now." She looked into LaBounty's eyes in a great fiery manner.

Joe's eyes flashed and his body stiffened. He sat up straight, clumsily buttoning up his shirt. "Doc, wrap up my arms as best you can. Mrs. Prettyman, spread the word. Everybody ought to right now get over in front of the office here so's I can talk to them." Annabelle lifted her dress and rushed away. "Kaymaki, when I give the word I want you down at the school to take charge of the kids and wait for my orders. Take Charlie with you."

Kaymaki looked to want to ask a hundred questions but kept still, prepared to do what she was told.

Joe spoke rapidly to Doctor Finch while the young man bound his arms. "Doc, hire yourself some deputies from among the womenfolk, gather up all your doctor stuff, and hightail it over to the school. We're going to set up headquarters there." Kaymaki's school was on the extreme southeast end of town, and as far away from the fire as it was possible to get and still be in town. It was also directly adjacent to the Soo Line Depot.

"Mr. Cayo," Joe continued. "Get to anyone that still has a running automobile and have them to form up at the livery. Get all your own cars out and ready. Nobody leaves till my say so." Percy was on his way before Joe finished.

Joe LaBounty fell silent, a faraway look in his eyes. He sat there on Doc Finch's table for quite a spell--or so it seemed to the others--staring at something only he could see. At length, he slapped on his hat, raking the brim even with a practiced move. He adjusted his pistol belt and stepped outside.

At first, the people that were gathering took no notice of him. They were thoroughly preoccupied, murmuring among themselves and glancing to the northwest, all the while pawing the dirt with fidgety feet. Each was secretly hoping their sons, brothers, fathers, and husbands would right now abandon the fight north of town, show their faces this very minute, and together they would jump into their automobiles and wagons and flee. Get away from this awful horror that had descended upon them and their town. Forget the idea of trying to save our worldly goods; it is time to save our lives!

What the good folks of Balsam were not at all thinking about was the man who came out of the doctor's office and onto the boardwalk. He said nothing, simply stood there, waiting for everyone to one-by-one stop talking among themselves and look his way. When each by his turn finally did face him and saw it was Joe LaBounty standing on the walk, their expressions changed to a profound remorse over what they had put him through. Despite the great crisis, the stunning news of his complete innocence had flashed through the village. Nobody quite knew what to make of it.

A child shattered the eerie silence when she suddenly noticed Joe and pointed at him in alarm. "Look! Look!"

The youngster's mother immediately shushed the girl, never mind when the woman glanced up at LaBounty, her own countenance suggested she might easily have uttered the same exclamation.

For it *was* quite a sight, the first time the greater part of them had gotten a good look at Joe LaBounty since he'd been run off. He didn't appear at all the way they remembered him. He was somehow taller, leaner, tougher... and awful "broke in." Only a handful of the townspeople had ever seen him without his big coat on.

Many actually drew a step back; not a few womenfolk had their hands up to their mouths gasping silent O's. Annabelle Prettyman looked up at Joe, and the hair prickled on the nape of her neck. The fellow staring down at her and the others was not at all the same man that had come to her home only the day before. That was a broken man, without prospects, without will, without hope. This man was very different; *this man she had never met.*

The Montana hat, the one that had always looked so overlarge, so almost comical, was somehow diminished, did not overpower its owner as it had before. It was now a dirty little item, mostly crushed, hardly worth a mention. She studied his deeply-lined brown face and found only a mask, whatever thinking and feeling going on behind it unknowable. His arms were bleeding afresh, as were the areas around scores of B-B holes that had peppered his shirt. Joe LaBounty gave no notice of these wounds, did not seem to notice the hurt, was in a different place than those who gazed up at him.

Without having even come close to absorbing these shocks, the people of Balsam were confronted with yet another. What every set of eyes locked on to, what left the boys and girls wide-eyed and even a little frightened, was Joe LaBounty's unconcealed, old-fashioned gun belt.

It had a decidedly Spanish look, an unusual hand-dyed blue leather with fine border tooling that nicely set off the several silver medallions and shiny belt buckle. The twenty-four narrow bullet loops spaced around the belt gave the .45 caliber cartridges the illusion of being larger than they actually were. A rich-looking latigo tie down held the holster tightly in place.

Most compelling was the scroll-engraved Colt itself; still

gleamingly polished, even after all it had been through--a remarkable testament to the unfailing attentions of its owner. The grip was mother-of-pearl ivory, with the Mexican emblem on one side and the name 'LaBounty' carefully carved on the other. It appeared almost a dandy's piece, what some might call a Nancy rig. But notwithstanding its eerie beauty, the almost artful pairing of weapon and accessories to that particular hip, it was clear to all it was an instrument of death. And the man who wielded the tool was a master craftsman.

Annabelle recalled years ago seeing men like this one. She recollected seeing the same reactions from folks, the same distancing, the same respect mixed with fear. She conjured up an image of what must have been an epic shootout with Krieg Dabek. Odd. So very odd. Mrs. Prettyman had thought his kind were extinct.

Joe LaBounty was a gunfighter.

12:32 P.M.
Soo Line Bridge Northwest Of Balsam

The last timber, a limbed but unpeeled freshly cut popple, was on its way up the steep bank. The two older, suited men on whose backs it rode were breathing heavily. Mustering up what sounded like their last ounce of strength, Mr. Weyerhaeuser and Mr. Coy set the tree into place. Two younger men with mauls spiked it in.

The popple, or poplar, made good paper but it was a pitiful excuse for a structural timber on account of its very soft, fibrous wood. It never would have been used for such a thing if it wasn't all there was to be had. The kind of wood more properly used in mining and bridge work had long ago been cut away. Not for the first time did Art Easterday wonder where in the world this fire was getting enough fuel to do the kind of damage it was proceeding to do. Went to show, he could only conclude, how much had been left behind for waste and weeds.

Art Easterday clapped a sweat-drenched Mr. Weyerhaeuser on the back. "O.K. That's got it. Everybody back to the train. Time to let the tail go with the hide!" Art signaled the engineer.

Bucholtz was watching through his left side bench window and immediately started steam coursing through the engine. The last of the men clambered aboard as the train chuffed forward. With everyone holding their breath, the locomotive slowly crossed the bridge. It felt for a second like the span was about to buckle but it must have been Easterday's imagination, for nothing happened. He watched the caboose from the top of the tender, breathing a deep sigh of relief when it cleared the trestle.

Easterday took a place on the fireman's bench while the stoker worked to build steam. The conductor glanced out the window and looked over his right shoulder in the direction of the forest fire, very much like an outlaw might look back after a vigilante committee. Whoever was left in Balsam better be ready to move fast, because his train wasn't going to be there very long. They passed the one mile marker and Bucholtz blew the steam whistle for all it was worth.

12:39 P.M.
The Boardwalk In Front Of Doc Finch's Office

Despite the din and confusion that seemed to now be a permanent part of their lives, everyone heard the train whistle. They had been waiting, indeed praying, for it. Only minutes before, Joe had released the caravan of fully loaded automobiles with instructions to get away as fast as the machines would allow. Not a second could be spared, for parts of the forest fire were moving at an even greater rate than the speediest automobile.

LaBounty would not let them go until every single vehicle had been packed solid with people. There was no order at all to the loading, an unfortunate process very nearly resembling Darwin's theory of "survival of the fittest." Several times Joe had to wave his revolver at folks who were panicking to get in what were already overloaded cars, or were not allowing children to board up. With all of that, amongst all the terrible confusion, he still had to discharge his weapon to get them to finally move out.

Although 150 people had been evacuated, most folks were still left behind, along with scores of outlying refugees who continued to pour into town. Joe found it disturbing there were so many children with them; he thought he had gotten most of the young people out in the cars. There were also the families of the small army of firefighters still out in the field, who refused to leave without their men. Joe cursed under his breath. The fellows should have given up the fight ten or fifteen minutes ago.

"O.K., old man Schmeissing had it right," Joe said in a loud voice, so that even those in the back could be reassured. "The train is on its way. Let's get to it."

Schmeissing was a wonder. He had been beating his way to town, having holed up in his shack and scoffing at the danger until nearly too late, when he came across the Soo Line train. The awful wind and approaching fire had him so rattled he did not try to talk to the trainmen. But he did have the presence of mind to realize they were trying to fix the bridge and that it was a rescue train. Sketchy as the old codger's information was, it had been enough for Joe to put together a makeshift evacuation plan.

Joe ended his instructions to the townspeople without allowing any questions. There wasn't time; either everyone would have to know their job or that was that. The crowd broke up with a wave of his hand and everyone ran for the school and depot. He was careful to conceal it, but he had been very apprehensive. If the train could not get through, that would have been the end, for there was no other alternative; if it had not made it over the bridge none of what he had planned would matter. He shuddered at the image of the refugees being cut down while out in the open, at the vision of Kaymaki and Charlie being destroyed. He had been sorely tempted to put them in an automobile, but finally concluded that would be dishonorable. And Joe LaBounty had gotten a bellyful of dishonor. Besides, there was nary a doubt in his mind Kaymaki would refuse to leave in any event.

LaBounty was himself about to make for the schoolhouse when an incredible blast of wind raked the downtown, blowing hundreds of firebrands over the buildings. At least ten structures erupted into flames. Amidst great shouting and clatter, the firefighters burst from out of the smoky maelstrom. They were in utter and complete flight.

Joe shouted over and over as the men swept by him. "Head for the schoolhouse! To the schoolhouse!"

He could not tell whether they heard him or not, but their natural inclination seemed to be carrying them in generally the right direction. By Joe's rough count, at least four score men had come by him; probably others were streaming in from different directions.

LaBounty ran into the street and collared one of the stragglers. "How many left out there?"

The fellow was gagging for breath. "Don't know," he managed to say.

"What about injuries? Did you leave any men behind?" Joe's big left hand had the fellow's arm in a vise-grip and the man squirmed from the pressure.

"It's awful bad," the firefighter gasped. "Lots hurt. I saw mebbe half dozen corpses..." He tried to free himself. "Lemme go! We gotta get out of here! I don't wanna die!"

The man's eyes rolled wild and Joe saw it was hopeless. He let the fellow go and half-turned to follow, was past ready himself to get out of the hellhole that had been Balsam, when a solitary figure stumbled out of the smoke bank.

Father Thornton staggered up to Joe and went down on one knee, leaning heavily against the spade in his hands. His breathing was raspy and there were large globs of very red blood coming from out of his mouth. Joe immediately deduced he had severe internal injuries.

"No hope," the priest rasped. "We're doomed." He was at the end of his rope.

The half-breed felt not a shred of pity. Joe LaBounty was a man who held a grudge, an individual altogether capable of taking revenge against those who would harm him or his people. While Joe completely disliked Gordie Patterson, he could at least comprehend the dead constable's actions, could see that what he did was guided by self-interest and advancement. That was human frailty, ugly but understandable. The man at Joe's feet, however, was entirely another matter. The Roman Catholic cleric had shown himself to be thoroughly intolerant, mean-spirited, and unforgiving toward the Ojibway. He had persecuted those Indians who continued to practice the old religion, even turning Joe's own mother against the Manitous. This so-called holy man had openly stated the Anishinabe were subhumans, that unless they could be totally remade in the white man's image they were worthy only of extermination.

For this particular one, this so-called "priest," Joe Labounty held in his heart a loathing so profound he was incapable of expressing it. It was all he could do to keep from raising his hand and striking the man down. To count coup on an enemy of his people one more time.

But he suddenly went another way, snarling, "What is your angry God mad about now, Thornton? Is He so shallow and weak He takes His own people for no reason? What fable can you make up to explain this!"

THE DEVIL'S HOLIDAY

Labounty's bile rose and he forgot himself, forgot his responsibility to the citizens of Balsam, forgot the danger to Charlie and Kaymaki, forgot the risk to his own life. Hate had bit hard and the venom coursed through his veins.

"Can you hear it, Thornton? Hear the crackle, the hiss! The roar! Is that the sound of your God laughing?"

Thornton was beside himself with confusion and fear, and it was too much. "He has forsaken me," the priest said mechanically. "He has forsaken me."

A huge explosion rent the town. Ostertag's store, full of tree-clearing dynamite, had blown up. Splinters of wood and debris cascaded down on LaBounty and Father Thornton. Joe's face became so hot it felt like he was standing next to a blast furnace. He tied a bandanna around his nose and mouth and hunched down next to the kneeling Thornton. The smoke had become so thick Joe's eyes watered continuously and he could hardly breathe. Yet, he made no move to leave. He wanted to watch the man, wanted to see what would happen next. Something was about to happen.

The priest gasped, sucking in even more of the toxic air. His eyes grew wild. He flailed his arms and hands in front of him, as if to ward off yet another affliction, another demon. His body shuddered uncontrollably in what was unmistakably a death throe. Of a sudden, Father Thornton staggered to both feet and faced the holocaust. Like an Old Testament prophet, he raised his arms to embrace the Host, speaking one last time.

"Behold the Devil's Holy Day!"

12:40 P.M.
At The Schoolhouse

Mrs. Prettyman had collected what would be the Upper Room children and was attempting to calm them with a story suggested by Kaymaki. L. Frank Baum's fantasy about the wondrous land of Oz had seemed a subject as far away from their current predicament as was possible to get. Kaymaki, Miss Kelley, and Charlie were in what would be the Lower Room doing their best to calm the little ones and to explain what was expected of them. It had to be drummed into their heads, in case they got separated from an adult.

Fighting back tears that Kaymaki knew were for his lost family, a game Charlie told the children to be brave, that everything would be O.K., and don't worry, Mr. LaBounty will pull us through. He was a real lawman, Charlie said, who took on the meanest outlaw there ever was and beat him. They listened and looked in wide-eyed wonder when he pulled back the bandage on his leg to show them where he had been shot by Krieg Dabek. Kaymaki stood with arms folded, looking on with a certain maternal pride at Mr. Olaf "Charlie" Haakonson, who was this morning a boy but was now a man.

The schoolhouse and yard was a mass of humanity. People that had been injured laid in the boy's and girl's cloak rooms, where Doc Finch tended to them. A small corps of women were in the basement victualing folks. Teenaged girls race-coursed up and down the steps carrying sandwiches, coffee, milk, and water. The rest of the refugees were jammed on the school porch, or milling about the schoolyard, which was adjacent to the Soo Line track. The safety fence between the yard and track had been torn down.

Despite the tumult, there was a certain calmness. No one was shouting or generally having a duck-fit. People moved about purposefully. Folks paid heed to each other's space and acted civilly. The long lines at the school's two small privies were orderly. Yet the grim faces and tight-lipped nods, acknowledgements that confirmed to one another they still had hold of their humanity, could not conceal a great uneasiness. Kaymaki sensed the panic that lurked just below the surface.

Earlier, on the boardwalk at Doc Finch's, Joe had spoken to a few of the more stable older men to be on the lookout for when that moment came. When the thin veneer of civilized behavior crumbled. He had told them to be ready to act, forcefully if need be, to keep order. Joe talked as if the thing had already happened, that it was foreordained and could not be changed. That unless the men did not act to prevent it, terror would consume the people. Kaymaki was very much afraid Joe was right, for those same men were now brandishing weapons in the yard, giving orders that had but little justification than to keep folks on a short leash.

Kaymaki shook her head in dismay. If the townspeople did come unglued, what actually could be done? She could not imagine a situation where shots would be fired. Friends shooting friends, fathers gunning down sons-in-law, brothers against brothers? In the midst of a shared catastrophe? Unthinkable. No, she concluded, if people did lose their heads, the game would be up. The armed men would not fire at all, but would throw down their weapons and themselves be sucked into the general hysteria. Everyone would instinctively bolt to the southeast, would heedlessly fly into the swamps and woods in their desperation to get away from the fire. It would be every man and woman for themselves, with every thread of common human decency thrown to the winds. And surely all would die, for there was no way to outrun this fire by either foot or horse. Kaymaki had seen the folly of that reasoning at Lawler.

She exhaled heavily, massaging her temples in a doomed attempt to rub away a rare headache. The rescue train was their only chance. And the Balsam villagers simply had to keep their senses until it got here. That was all there was to it.

At that moment, Ostertag's general store exploded. Screams erupted from the Upper Room, the one closest to downtown. Kaymaki and everyone else in Lower rushed to join Mrs. Prettyman and the older children. As many as could pressed their noses against the north windows. What was once Balsam was now a fireball, a boiling orange-red mass floating in a swirling, gray-black void. To Kaymaki, it looked like the end of time.

A shrill yelp cut through the gloom. One of the little boys pointed excitedly at something silhouetted against the Dante-like background, at Joe LaBounty running toward the railroad siding.

12:41 P.M.
At The Schoolhouse

Three men led by Gunnar Torvald were on the schoolhouse roof scurrying from one end of the building to the other slapping wet gunny sacks and dumping buckets of water on the burning cedar shingles. Rayno Randa and Smitty were down below keeping the bucket brigade functioning and watching over the pump, which was powered by a windmill that provided water for both the school and nearby Soo Line Depot.

Within the last couple of minutes, the wind and heat from the burning town had become terrific. Several men in the brigade gang couldn't take it any longer. They threw down their buckets, bolted across the tracks and ran into the woods, effectively committing suicide.

There was another incredible whoosh from out of the inferno, carrying an even hotter breath. Old man Schmeissing's tattered clothes caught fire and Rayno Randa had to dump a bucket of water on him to get it out.

"Douse each other!" Randa yelled at the top of his lungs. "Everybody soak your clothes and move back!" He yelled at Gunnar Torvald to pull his men off the school roof.

The fire was on them. Rayno looked around for the man who was supposed to run to the school and give the signal for the children to make for the train, but he was nowhere to be seen. Randa's heart sank when he realized the fellow was one of the men who had fled into the forest.

Rayno was about to order the man next to him to make for

the school when a woman screamed and pointed up at a mill sail. It had broken loose and was flapping wildly in the wind. Rayno Randa tried desperately to brake the sails, but the sixty-mile-an-hour winds were spinning them so rapidly, he could not get the handle to engage. When finally the gearing did mesh, the stress on the cast iron parts was too great and the mechanism disintegrated.

Randa looked up at the dangerously swaying windmill. He yelled "Run!" She's going!" but his warning was smothered by the roar of the fire. Another massive blast of heat and wind slammed into the mill, knocking it completely loose of its moorings.

The good citizens below proceeded to go into a frenzy. Instead of using common sense and running away from the falling structure, they stampeded themselves into a mindless, milling ball. The forty-foot tall structure crashed to the ground, killing or injuring a dozen people.

12:43 P.M.
Upper Room

The "Wizard of Oz" slipped out of Mrs. Prettyman's hands and dropped to the floor when the windmill crashed. The screams from the injured were agonizing; somehow the sounds pierced the school walls, even over the incredible background din. The children looked at each other in shock and several began to whimper anew.

"Hush, children. It will be all right," Mrs. Prettyman lied.

Despite her town-gossip reputation, lying, especially to children, did not come naturally to Annabelle. Throughout her own childhood she had been constantly victimized by prevarication. And with Nathan, in business settings, she was often required to stretch the truth, in order to avoid alienating current or potential customers. It was something she had never been comfortable with or very good at it. In this particular case, however, the words had come easily enough. She was determined to shield these poor innocents from the awfulness for as long as she could, for as long as she still breathed.

Annabelle Prettyman had now taken leave of any illusion that she would live through this fire. It had come to her in the last few moments, as a certainty, as a known thing. As if it had been chiseled in stone. She could take some cold comfort, she grimly decided, that at least she had beaten Dabek. It was going to take a much bigger monster than him to finish her off.

Clutching two trembling young hands, Mrs. Prettyman drank in the scenes of these, her final minutes. She glanced around the school room, carefully examining everything within her field of view. Her eye caught scores of little items she would never have noticed had her senses not been in a heightened condition--a hairline plaster crack near the regulator clock, cobwebs in the corner above the roll-down map rack, spitball encrustations on the ceiling, a fragment of a lesson for the fifth grade on the blackboard. Soon, very soon, all of it would be gone, would be transformed into something else, never to be as it was before.

Mrs. Prettyman abruptly stopped her inspection. She stared hard at the ten foot high wall next to her, the solid east wall of the school.

She had been through this before, in 1871, in Chicago. During the Great Fire. When a burning wall was about to fall and her mother saved her life at the last second by pushing her away. What an astonishing thing that, lo these many years later, another fiery wall would loom over her, ready to bring her life full circle!

Mrs. Prettyman could not help but note a certain poetry to it, an air of destiny. Considering the circumstances, she found herself quite matter-of-fact and strangely calm. The terror that had since childhood gripped her whenever she was around any kind of fire, the great waves of fear that had held her captive for the last hour, slowly ebbed away.

Annabelle let out a little oh, almost smiling. The children looked at her queerly. Mrs. Nathan Dexter Prettyman had just remembered today was her 58th birthday. Considering her very unpromising start in this old world, and all the rocks in the road since, that was not so bad a mark.

12:43 P.M.
On The Rescue Train

Easterday's stomach had twisted into knots when the windmill smashed into the throng. He carefully scanned the area around the school, yard, and depot for any signs of life, but saw only smoke and fire. Beyond, the village of Balsam was nearly gone. From where he stood, he could not imagine how anyone could be still alive; it occurred to him the windmill may have finished off what few were left.

He rubbed the stubble on his chin with authority, inadvertently producing a raspberry. Perhaps he ought not continue to slow down, should not put the volunteers and all the other refugees he had rescued in even more jeopardy, but instead tell Bucholtz to highball her right on through to Kettle River. Get out now, not put at risk the entire train for the remote chance of saving a few more souls.

He was mulling the matter over when scores of terrified human beings emerged from behind a smoke cloud and broke for Balsam's siding. He could see them pointing excitedly at his train. A gust, another heat blast from Balsam, momentarily cleared the view, revealing many more people running from the schoolyard.

Something was moving on the track up ahead. Art yelled at the engineer, "See there Bucholtz!" A man was swinging a lamp right and left across the track, the railroad signal for DANGER - STOP.

"Do you suppose the track is gone?" the engineer asked

nervously. The train continued to slow, but was still moving at a fairly rapid rate.

Easterday pointed to the right, at the siding. "No, look there." Gangs of men were swarming over eight or ten empty tie and cordwood cars. Art slapped his knee. "They figured good, knew we'd be full to the gizzard." He moved close to Bucholtz, taking the engineer's arm in his excitement. "Stop the train just past the siding switch!"

Bucholtz wrestled loose of the hold, looking like a man who had just busted a gut. "Hell, there's no time for that," he shouted. "The fire is already on top of us. Let those that can jump on do it when we roll through but we ain't stopping!" He nodded at his ash eater to shovel more coal into the firebox, then manipulated the regulator handle to increase the steam going into the cylinders.

Notwithstanding Conductor Easterday's Christian principles, he was no mollycoddle. Twenty-one-year-old Able Bodied Seaman Arthur Kilsworth Easterday had been with Commodore George Dewey when the American fleet defeated the Spanish at Manila Bay. He was a man steeped in the notions of gallantry, one of the Northern Pacific's most respected conductors, a Captain on the road's premier transcontinental passenger route. Abandoning the people of Balsam to a certain death was out of the question.

Easterday reached under his vest to a homemade armpit holster and drew out a .22 Caliber Iver Johnson Petite Hammerless. He had carried this relatively rare "gentlemen's" sidearm ever since getting beat to within an inch of his life by three drunk Montana cowboys who refused to pay their fare. Easterday held the weapon to Engineer Gust Bucholtz's head, the barrel barely protruding past his fist. "Stop this train and take up those cars or I will pull this trigger, so help me God!"

12:43 P.M.
Inside The Schoolhouse

From the entry foyer window, Kaymaki watched the train roll in, and all the many people running for it. There was furious activity getting the Balsam cars ready. She could only hope and pray the men could get them hooked to the train before it was too late.

Suddenly, Kaymaki stepped back, her neck prickling. She dashed into the Upper Room. All the children were glued to the many-paned north front, the windowed wall that was all that separated them from the advancing flames. Kaymaki's mouth dropped open in stupefaction, as if she had been in a trance and only just now came to her senses.

This was all wrong! What are we still doing here? Why are we not racing for the train? Why are we not fleeing the fire! They had become mesmerized, acting like spectators instead of participants in the great drama.

Joe had ordered Kaymaki to wait for the order to evacuate the children to the train. The instructions had been firm--wait for the man he had designated to come to the school and give the signal, so as not to prematurely expose the young ones to the wind, smoke, firebrands, heat, and any other hazard between the school and the siding. And that was precisely what she had done. Kaymaki now realized with a terrible finality that no such signal was ever going to come in time.

She screamed at the children. "Get back from the windows!" She ran up to the main clutch of young ones. "Run for the train! Run!"

The startled pupils looked at their teacher in confusion. They saw no immediate threat, no reason for alarm. After all, their faces seem to say, the fire is out there, beyond the windows--are we not safe in our little school? Were we not told to wait for the signal?

Kaymaki screamed at them again, in the angriest voice they

had ever heard her use. That finally knocked sense into them and they bolted for the main door. As if on cue, the Malevolence caused to pass a large air pressure change inside the classroom, which sucked out most of the atmosphere. The entire north wall, the structurally weakest side, imploded with a shattering blast, showering the classroom with glass and debris.

In that last instant before the north wall disintegrated, Mrs. Prettyman also comprehended what was happening. She grabbed a small girl, the youngster nearest to her, and protectively wrapped herself around the child. The two took the blast together and were launched fifteen feet through the air, impacting against the roll-up partition separating Upper and Lower.

Before the last board had dropped from the ceiling, before the last shard of glass had come loose and broken on the floor, before the gallons of dust buried behind the walls had even started to settle, there arose the most deafening roar Kaymaki had ever heard. Half-buried under rubble and stunned to the point of not knowing if she was injured or not, it sounded for all the world like Armageddon.

Kaymaki had every reason to be awestruck, for she and the others were about to witness something that few had seen, and no one comprehended. The chief difference between small and large fires is not so much the size of the area affected as the dynamics within the larger fire itself. On rare occasions, a "large" fire reaches a certain heat and intensity, and demands to change the rules. When this occurs, a vertical convective current is created. This rapidly heated air rises and heavier cooler air, which can only come from where the fire is going, races in to fill the gap. More fresh air rushes in, is heated and rises, sustaining the cycle. All this is happening at an ever accelerating pace, upsetting the atmosphere for miles around. The increasingly voracious fireline begins to "lean" heavily into its fuel--wood and oxygen--blowing out firebrands ahead of it. These burning chunks of debris cause more fires, which immediately form new convection columns, creating huge companion fires. Of a sudden, all these parties coalesce and there is a stupendous blow-up, accompanied by a hurricane of fire as much out of human control as an exploding star. In a later time, when phenomena of this nature became better understood, a Balsam-type event would become known as a firestorm.

12:45 P.M.
Balsam Siding

After detaching the caboose, the rescue train huffed past the siding switch. The Balsam cars were immediately brought out. Three four-horse teams had been hooked up in tandem to shunt the empty cars on to the mainline, with scores of men helping things along by pushing as best they could. It was very hard work to get the dead weight to moving, but once they got it rolling it went a little easier. It helped the siding was slightly uphill from the mainline. When the last Balsam car cleared the siding, Bucholtz's switchman reset the junction blades. The Balsam cars were quickly attached to the train and the caboose was rolled forward and reconnected.

A gang of men led by Conductor Easterday and Mr. Weyerhaeuser took immediate charge of loading the Balsam refugees, who were in an absolute frenzy to get aboard. Many people were injured for no other reason than the person next to them lost control of his or herself. The bad footing also hindered the process; boots and shoes were slipping on the cinder ballast and folks kept tumbling down into the track-bed drainage ditch. The high winds and overall background noise made voice communication virtually impossible.

Some of the Balsam people tried to get into the rescue train boxcars, which were already full of refugees from up the line.

Easterday was going out of his mind trying to convince them to get into their own cars. They ignored his pleas, climbing up the iron rung ladders to the car top, or sliding "hobo style" onto the truss rods underneath. Several of the latter would be injured or killed before the day was out. Easterday finally gave up trying to help those hotheads and ran back to aid Weyerhaeuser with the loading of folks into the Balsam cars. He could see already they were filling up, and that they had a new problem.

Easterday addressed it the best he could, moving down the cars, yelling, "No baggage! Save room for your neighbor! Throw the grips overboard!"

He was disappointed but not surprised when no one took him up. Not one man, woman, or child was willing to give up their handful of possibles, what very few possessions they still had in this world. Every satchel, every pack, every grip, was clutched in a manner that suggested for all the world they were filled with gold nuggets. Conductor Easterday continued to work his way down the train, barking orders right and left, resigned to do what he could.

12:45 P.M.
On Top Of The School

When the windmill collapsed, the shock wave knocked over the ladder to the schoolhouse roof and Gunnar Torvald had to shinny down a drainpipe. He had no more than hit the ground when he heard/felt the heat/shock wave that walloped the school. Unsure what had happened or what to do, he could only react to the threat before him. He had seen the windmill crash and he could hear people screaming. Gunnar sprinted toward the mill wreckage. Toward Rayno Randa and the others still trapped there.

12:46 P.M.
At The Wreckage Of The Windmill

The two men's eyes met briefly, warily, neither sure of how to take the other. True they had been working "together" on the school roof fire, but this was the first they had been this close to one another. Rayno had watched Torvald as he nearly single-handedly kept the schoolhouse from burning. The Finn admired how the big man had given of himself without thought to his own safety. How he had bought time for the children until the train arrived.

Rayno had finally accepted how terribly wrong he'd been about Gunnar Torvald. The Finn had been the hard case, the one who couldn't see the truth. He was the problem, he the stubborn Suomi. Rayno wanted awful bad to say he was sorry, to tell Gunnar it was all a desperate mistake. But there wasn't time; the Master of the Fire had charge of the clock now.

The Swede knelt beside him and instantly sized up the problem. Randa's legs-- they were both bruised but Rayno thought not broken--were pinned. Torvald squeezed Rayno's shoulder and stood up. A number of men were standing around, having narrowly missed being crushed themselves and not at all able to shake off the fog they were in.

"You!" Torvald barked, pointing at one of them. "And you and you. Clear away junk!"

There was nothing quite like having an angry Gunnar Torvald yell at a fellow to wake him up. The men tore at the debris like they were possessed--all of them jumped in--and very quickly had the mill free of obstacles. Gunnar directed individual "volunteers" to grab hold of Rayno and the others still tangled in the wreckage. After positioning several men to help with the lifting, the big Swede came around and shouldered a twelve-inch thick pine member.

With a mighty voice, he thundered, "One, two, t'ree, HEAVE!"

Torvald's bellow metamorphosed into an agonizing grunt as the mill timbers rose ever so slightly. It was no more than an inch or two, but that was enough. Rayno and the others were yanked free.

Gunnar relaxed the pressure on the timber and the mill settled heavily back to earth. While catching his breath, something caught the Swede's eye. Randa turned to see what it was. There was a fellow at the schoolhouse steps, tearing away at the jumble of boards, lath, and plaster like a madman. Joe LaBounty was trying to break through to the trapped children.

12:50 P.M.
At The Schoolhouse Door

After barely escaping the inferno in town, it had taken every ounce of will power Joe LaBounty could summon not to run directly for the school. He could tell as he ran for the siding--Joe saw their frightened little faces pressed against the window glass--that the children were still there. He was staggered by the realization the signal had not been given, that his precaution to protect the young people had not worked and they were still inside the building.

He had no doubt but what Kaymaki was also still there, for she would never abandon the children. As anguished as he was at the horrifying idea he might still lose her, his primary responsibility, his first duty, was to see to the evacuation, make sure the refugees were loaded so the pullout could proceed. Those in the school would have to wait; his Honor demanded it. In an agony almost as great as his own disgrace, Joe had put his head down and made for the train.

He saw straightaway there was a strong man running the loading, a train conductor who it was plain had deduced Joe's plan. The cars LaBounty had ordered readied were already hooked up and ready to go. Under the crisp orders of the conductor and another big, well-dressed customer, folks were scrambling aboard. A profoundly relieved Joe LaBounty took off for the schoolhouse like he was Jim Thorpe.

He had struggled through the junk on the steps and was battering at the door with a chunk of timber when a man rushed by him and slammed into it with all the force of a crazed bull. The door casing disintegrated and it, the door, and Gunnar Torvald burst into the entry foyer. Joe followed the Swede past the cloak rooms and a small crushed table that had held the cedar water bucket. Although neither man knew it, Gunnar stepped on the boy's tin dipper and Joe the girl's, crushing them both. Ignoring cuts and scratches from nails and wood splinters, they crawled over the rubble toward the screaming and shouting coming from the Upper Room. By now, the building was thoroughly on fire and there was a lot of smoke. All of the children were either coughing or crying. LaBounty heard a weak voice from the far corner.

"Joe, over here."

It was Kaymaki. She was tugging at her left leg, having caught it under a jumble of desks. Joe looked up. Above her head was a portion of the burning roof that had separated from the rest of the structure. It was swinging back and forth, as if on a hinge.

On the other side of the room, Gunnar was throwing children out the glassless windows. The room was about eight feet off the ground and there was no ladder handy, so Torvald was dropping one after another into the waiting hands of other rescuers, other brave souls, the real *men* of the community, stout fellows who had taken note of the situation. Cut, bruised, and bleeding from their many hours on the fireline, they were still able, *willing*, to put other lives ahead of their own. They had seen Torvald break for the school and followed him.

Gunner moved like a well-oiled machine and the schoolroom rapidly emptied. It helped that the children had the good sense to position themselves to advantage once they understood what was happening. Remarkably, there had been few serious injuries among them, owing chiefly to Kaymaki's warning. Some of the older kids fled out the door Gunnar had broken down, while others were jumping out the windows on their own. As they had been instructed, all the youngsters made a beeline for the tracks. Get on train! Gunnar was yelling at the top of his lungs, no matter what, get on train!

Joe needed only a second or two to take in Torvald's work, to know the big man had the children's removal well in hand. LaBounty turned back to the far corner, to Kaymaki and the hinged roof. He had been away from her for only seconds but in that brief span, the loose roof had ruptured further, and it was now hanging by a splinter. He could not possibly reach her before it tore loose; the detritus of chairs, desks, two by fours, plaster, lath, and dust was everywhere and there was no path through it to where she was. Joe waved at her in a pitiful sort of way, making agonizing little noises and hopping from one foot to the other. He could not have been more distraught over his impotence.

While Joe sputtered helplessly, Charlie Haakonson materialized next to Kaymaki. The boy's clothes and face were white from plaster powder, and there was a rivulet of red down one cheek caused by a nail slash to his scalp. Favoring his wounded leg, he swung himself into position next to Kaymaki and lunged forward. At that moment, the roof gave way.

Balsam, like most country schools, fastened individual school desks on wood rails that rested on the floor. This arrangement provided stability and kept the desks lined up in proper fashion, no small matter considering the type of rambunctious youngsters customary to these kinds of schools. Any number of desks could be joined together, but three was usual, in that it offered the desired balance and was still not so heavy that a couple of strong boys couldn't move them around.

It was one of these seat sections that had Kaymaki pinned and that Charlie attacked.

Moving like a football player on a blocking assignment, young Haakonson had lowered a shoulder and slammed against a cast iron desk support, tipping the debris-filled gang of seats up on one side. Kaymaki simultaneously jerked her leg free. The both of them rolled away as the ceiling crashed down on them. While the greater part of the roof missed, a chunk of shiplap struck Kaymaki and she screamed. Charlie was hammered by a two-by-four joist and didn't move. Moments later, Joe was beside them both, after half-rolling, half-crawling, half-falling over all the junk.

Beyond the school walls, somewhere to the southeast, LaBounty heard a long, faint steam whistle. It took a moment for it to register what it was. The train was pulling out. The rescue train was leaving. They were going to be left behind.

LaBounty wrestled an unconscious Charlie over his shoulders in a fireman's carry and picked up Kaymaki in his arms. It was no easy task; he had to favor most of her weight on his left side on account of his shot-up right side was nearly useless, never mind his left arm was still rickety from Dabek's bale hook. Joe saw there was a side door only a few feet away. They could get out that way and make a run for it.

Something made him look back. Perhaps a sound, a shadow, a sixth sense, something. The children were all gone, but near the roll-up partition between upper and lower--he could only just barely see through the screen of smoke and dust--there were people who still hadn't gotten out. He made out a man standing over a woman and small child. The woman had one arm around the child and the other around a great oak of a leg. It was Mrs. Prettyman and Gunnar Torvald.

The Swede had gone back for them, had come to take her and the little girl out after seeing to the rescue of all the other children. He could have fled honorably, been proclaimed a hero; no one would have ever known the difference, known that he had left people behind.

Except Gunnar Torvald. He had remained within the burning bowels of the school because Mrs. Prettyman and the child were still trapped and his job was not done.

And there the great lumberjack stood, anchored to his post. For a split-instant, Joe could not understand why the big man made no attempt to gather up the woman and child and flee. Then he saw. There was no place to go, the entire roof from that part of the building was collapsing. Was already coming down, was only feet above their heads, falling, falling.

Joe stood transfixed. The Swede had not flinched, not even, Joe believed, batted an eye. Not even as he stood on the edge of eternity. In the very last instant, Gunnar Torvald threw back his head, jutted out his jaw, and protectively threw both arms straight up, palms out. The three of them blinked out, as if someone had pulled the chain on an electric light.

12:57 P.M.
On The Rescue Train Caboose

Rayno Randa jumped up and down, pointing toward the school. "Stop the train! I see someone coming!" He kept shouting and pointing. "It must be Gunnar! Stop the train!"

Randa looked back and forth between Conductor Easterday and the oncoming figure, his eyes pleading. Art stared at Rayno like the Finlander was two sandwiches short of a picnic. The weary conductor had already chosen to ignore several running figures waving desperately as the train pulled away from them. "Not a chance son," was all Art could say, not able to bring himself to look where Randa had been pointing.

Easterday was very much afraid they had waited too long and would not be able to clear the town in time. He hoped the men were getting all the fires out on top the boxcars and that everyone had kept the windows closed. All they needed now was for firebrands, or even the oven-like radiated heat, to set the wood cars on fire. He thought about all the Balsam people exposed on the open tie cars. He took out his handkerchief and wiped the sweat from his forehead. There was nothing he could do for them; they would simply have to take their chances.

Easterday had waited until the last second before giving the signal to Bucholtz. He had put Mr. Weyerhaeuser up there with the engineer, in order to ensure the man did not try to leave early. Mr. Weyerhaeuser caught on to the problem immediately and made it very clear to Mr. Bucholtz there wouldn't be any of that.

Art leaned on the guard rail and looked down at the track bed from the caboose's rear platform. While the heavy train was building up speed, the sleepers were still receding very slowly. He listlessly glanced to the side, as it happened in the direction where Randa had been pointing, and suddenly through the smoke saw a desperate Joe LaBounty making for the train.

Easterday stood bolt upright. "My God!" he exclaimed. "It's one man carrying two people."

Randa raced to the platform guard rail for his own look, and promptly slumped his shoulders. "They ain't never going to make it," he said sourly. His tone made clear his disappointment it wasn't Gunnar Torvald.

Art looked crossly at the Finn. "Quick, get some men. He's coming strong. They might have a chance."

12:58 P.M.
Thirty Feet From The Moving Train

Joe LaBounty's need for oxygen was so acute his vision blurred. It felt like his lungs would burst. The smoke-charged air, coupled with the tremendous effort necessary to run and carry Charlie and Kaymaki at the same time, was taxing his body to the positive limit. Yet he had to keep moving, had to keep pumping his legs. He could not allow himself to think of anything else, had to focus his mind totally in support of his legs. It was the only chance for any of them.

Joe had gotten an angle on the caboose, the only thing that gave him hope. To have had to chase it all the way straight down the track, as he was forced to do now, would have spelled the end. He would have stopped--not because he wanted to but because his mind would have no longer been able to lash his legs beyond endurance, to force them to keep going, to make them do the impossible. As they were very nearly doing now.

It was going to be a close thing. Although the train was slowly picking up speed, the only reason it wasn't already too late was because of the tremendous load the 4-6-2 was being asked to pull. Joe could now make out the faces of the men on the caboose's rear platform. They were waving at him through the smoke, shouting encouragement.

"Run, man. Run!" he heard one of them shouting.

Red-hot pokers stabbed at Joe's calf muscles. He began to hallucinate, and for a terrifying moment he thought the blaze had caught up with him and his backside was on fire. He was only a few feet away from the rear platform, but it might as well have been a mile. He wasn't closing the gap anymore. He could see the train slipping away, feel his will going with it, suddenly gripped with the realization he was going to lose the race. That he, Charlie, and Kaymaki were going to die. That this was the end. He stumbled on a tie and would have fallen if a man had not grabbed him.

The fellow put an arm around Joe's trunk and propelled him forward. Two other gents, leaning heavily over the caboose back-rail with several other men holding their legs, seized Joe's arms. LaBounty mouthed a silent scream from the incredible pain.

Many hands clutched at shoulders, trousers, hands, arms, skirts, belts, and buttocks. LaBounty felt himself pulled off his feet. With a whoop, the men yanked as one, and Joe, Kaymaki, Charlie, and Rayno Randa tumbled up and over the caboose rail.

1:10 P.M.
Aboard The Train

A panting Rayno Randa sat down Indian-style beside Joe LaBounty. The Finn was still shaking. He had slipped on the cinder ballast just as they were being pulled aboard and very nearly didn't make it himself.

Easterday had taken Kaymaki and Charlie inside the crummy and laid them down in sleeping bunks. They were both pretty banged up but breathing regular, though Charlie was still conked out. Doc Finch had been summoned.

"Gunnar?" Rayno asked.

Joe shook his head sadly, continuing to wrap strips of muslin around both his bleeding arms. The Finn stuck his head through the wrought iron back-rail and, one at a time, pressed his right forefinger against each nostril, blowing them clean on the track bed. Tears streamed down his face.

The two men sat alone on the caboose platform, looking northwest, looking back. The horizon was a thick band of orange fury sandwiched between an unearthly blackness above and below it. It was like watching Hell recede, as if they were in a ship sailing away from the Underworld. Joe became aware of the comforting *clickety-clackety* of the rails as the train accelerated, as it continued to speed them away from the nightmare. A regular sound, from a regular train, heading for a regular world.

Joe thought about the priest Thornton, about the man's last words. The devil's holiday, he'd called it. Joe snorted in a kind of half-laugh. It was the only thing LaBounty had ever heard the son-of-a-bitch say he agreed with.

EPILOGUE
One Month Later
Balsam Town Site

Joe LaBounty kicked through the pine ash, charcoaled cupboards, and blackened pots and pans of what had once been Mrs. Prettyman's kitchen. The fire had burned so hot there wasn't anything worth salvaging in the entire house. He kicked at the parlor silverware, plated not solid, he saw. It was a single, grotesque ingot.

Joe patted his pockets and came up with a bag of peanuts. He'd had a big breakfast, but his body had gone right through it and he was ravenous. He looked around as he chewed, tossing the bag over to Kaymaki before he had eaten all of the fruit.

Martial Law had been declared right after the fire and it had taken until now to get permission to come back. A few light-fingered folks had done their work, but mostly people had behaved themselves. Things weren't back to normal, by any stretch, but the pieces were getting picked up.

Kaymaki pointed at the quaint little necessary house, with its ivied trellis and brightly painted hues of blue, red, yellow, and green. It hadn't been touched, looking ready enough for Mrs. Prettyman to come on out for her morning constitutional. The firestorm had skipped over it; an odd thing that happened more often than many believed possible.

"Can you beat it?" Kaymaki said.

The three of them wandered about, kicking and poking. Charlie's crutches were getting black points from all the ash.

"It was a lovely home, Joe," Kaymaki said softly. "She was

so proud of it."

Joe took off his new Montana-peaked hat and made a grand sweeping gesture over the ruins. "We'll raise her up, Kaymaki. Better than before, and that's a promise." He added almost imperceptibly, looking far away. "To her."

In what had amounted to the single most momentous week of Joe LaBounty's life, there had arrived one more great surprise. On the morning of her last day, in gratitude for what Joe had done for her and perhaps with a premonition, Mrs. Nathan Dexter Prettyman had gone to the trouble of drawing up a Last Will and Testament. It had been found in good condition, inside her bodice, wrapped in an oilcloth. Her Aitkin lawyer pronounced the two-paragraph long, handwritten document bona fide--she had been careful to get it notarized--and informed Joe LaBounty he was the sole beneficiary of her estate. The attorney came as close to bowling Joe over as anyone ever had when he went on to say that in addition to her fully insured home in Balsam she owned negotiable securities worth in the neighborhood of one hundred thousand dollars.

LaBounty scanned the rubble that was once the thriving community of Balsam. Maybe a half dozen buildings still stood, if you could call it that, with the rest burned to the ground. The town fathers were getting ready to rebuild and most everybody had said they would return. Only this time the commercial buildings would be made out of brick, and all the latest developments in modern fireproofing would be adopted.

Except for a handful of folks that had gone to stay with relations, the community was now housed in temporary Red Cross shelters raised up in Moose Lake. They were simple, small frame structures, but entirely serviceable. Fire survivors were awful glad to get them, along with the medicine, food, and clothing that came from all over the state and nation. With winter coming on and all the livestock and crops lost, the real rebuilding would have to wait until spring.

One of the first things the citizens of New Balsam did was to elect themselves a town constable. They didn't actually need to vote on it; the council could have appointed one, but folks wanted to go on record. There was a good deal of healing that needed to go on all the way round. Of course, Joe LaBounty won unanimously. Everybody was pleased with themselves, figuring the action would go a long way toward making up for things.

Publicly, LaBounty appeared grateful, thanked everybody, and accepted the job. He gave every indication that bygones could be bygones. He couldn't afford not to, couldn't contemplate the idea of alienating Kaymaki, chance going off and wrecking everything all over again.

But the fact was, things were *not* right. Bygones were *not* bygones. Too much had happened. Joe could never forgive the townspeople for assuming his guilt, accepting the baseless charge on nothing more substantial than the color of his skin. At some point in the future, the whites were going to have to pay a higher price than simply buying him off.

What the Europeans would never be able to understand was that underneath Joe's fine new suit of clothes, behind his perfectly good command of the English language, beneath his understanding of their culture and values, and ultimately even transcending his own personal need for family and friends, was another man. With a secret life, on a sacred quest. A man only a handful of Anishinabes, those very few who remembered what a proud people they had been before the white man made them women, knew as Kills With His Hand.

This man was an unreconstructed Indian–Proud Warrior and Hunter, Unforgiver of Insults, and Merciless Avenger of Great Wrongs. The half of him known as Joe LaBounty, the civilized half that could live among the whites with a degree of peace, could perhaps forgive them. But Kills With His Hand... *Never!*

Joe took a deep breath and exhaled slowly. All that had to wait for a later time, after he had figured out a way to deal with the matter, for it was something Kaymaki would never understand or condone. He called Charlie to his side and put his arms around the young man. "Your room will be upstairs, right about here." He pointed at the rubble of the staircase Krieg Dabek had climbed.

Charlie looked at Joe in wonderment. "All to myself?" he asked.

Joe shrugged. "Well, there's old Jack. You want him to sleep out in the cold?"

Charlie shook his head emphatically, rubbing Jack's ears. The dog gratefully slobbered all over the young man's hands. Joe bent down and scratched the mutt's head, remembering the deep debt he owed the animal.

LaBounty pressed his advantage, serving up the molasses. "Another thing, you might as well figure on going to college because I've already decided the matter. A man can't get nowhere in this modern world without a good education." Charlie tried to whine, but his smile got in the way.

"And Mrs. LaBounty," Joe said to Kaymaki, grinning widely and pointing to the ground beneath his feet, "Our bedroom will be right here."

AUTHOR'S NOTES

The Cloquet-Moose Lake Fire of 1918 was one of the greatest disasters in American history. The event, largely obscured by the end of World War One and the Spanish Influenza Pandemic, was the nation's second worst forest fire, surpassed only by the 1871 Peshtigo, Wisconsin holocaust. On Columbus Day, 1918, a half a thousand Minnesotans were killed outright from burns, suffocation, and in an incredible auto pileup at what became known as Dead Man's Curve below Kettle River. Hundreds more fire sufferers perished from disease and influenza. Fifteen hundred square miles were burned, at least ten towns were completely obliterated (including Cloquet and Moose Lake), with another twenty communities (including Duluth) partially destroyed. Over 52,000 people were affected. For readers interested in learning more about this catastrophe, I recommend the book *The Fires Of Autumn* by Francis Carroll and Franklin Raiter (Minnesota Historical Society Press, St.Paul, MN, 55101).

While this yarn and the town of Balsam are fictional, many of the people and places portrayed were real. Ike Boekenoogen was the Aitkin County Sheriff at the time, and C.A. Maddy the county commissioner. Henry Blomberg still sleeps in the Argonne Forest. Simon and Mary Thompson headed a respected Ojibway family; Butch Phillips was the local strongman. Northern Pacific Agent Laurence Fauley and Great Northern Superintendent George Stewart are largely credited with providing trains in time to save the eight thousand people of Cloquet. Rudolph Weyerhaeuser and Sherman Coy were old-breed industrialists; I took the liberty of including them on

Art Easterday's train, when in fact they were back in Cloquet putting themselves in harm's way. Erline Kelley was one of the two teachers at Tamarack at the time; Mrs. Young the superintendent of schools. Burnquist was the governor and the wire to him from Mrs. Marcus (Mamie) Nelson actually occurred; the Home Guards arrived in the early afternoon and saved Tamarack. Dennis Carr went on to sue the railroad over the loss of his farm and won CARR VS DAVIS, which formed the basis for payment of thousands of claims.

There is a lot of old Tamarack in this story, people and places like the Beanery, Mrs. Ostertag's "blind-pig," mail carrier Dave Tweedy, Percy Cayo's livery, telephone operator Esther Steffer, the Haapoja's, the Maijala's, and Archie Cyrus' taxi service. And "Aunt Mamie" Nelson, as she was universally known. With her husband, Marcus, out fighting the fire and figuring the town was lost, she led a group of forty women and children, plus the soldiers, to her family farm just east of town to make their last stand. Fortunately for them, the firebreaks, a wind shift, and the soldier's brave fight along the fireline saved the town. The only serious loss was Marcus' huge sawmill and lumber yard complex, which was completely destroyed. It was a financial disaster of the first magnitude for the Nelsons, but the next day Mr. and Mrs. Nelson, their fourteen-year-old daughter and eleven-year-old son, and all the other people with them, were nearly giddy with relief that their lives had been spared.

One night about a decade and a half ago, at that same Tamarack farm, the Nelson daughter, then in her eighties, looked out a house window and saw a large swampgrass fire. While enough of a threat to buildings and livestock to keep many of us out fighting it most of the night, it never posed a serious risk to human life.

Yet my mother completely lost control of herself. In her own words, written in 1919, she was now and forever "completely terrified of any kind of fire." For survivors like Myrtle Nelson Harder, the memory of that horrific day never faded.

* * *